THE OTHER INSIDE

J.M. WHITE

Black Rose Writing | Texas

ISBN: 978-1-68433-417-9
PUBLISHED BY BLACK ROSE WRITING
www.blackrosewriting.com

Printed in the United States of America
Suggested Retail Price (SRP) $18.95

The Other Inside is printed in Baskerville

*As a planet-friendly publisher, Black Rose Writing does its best to eliminate unnecessary waste to reduce paper usage and energy costs, while never compromising the reading experience. As a result, the final word count vs. page count may not meet common expectations.

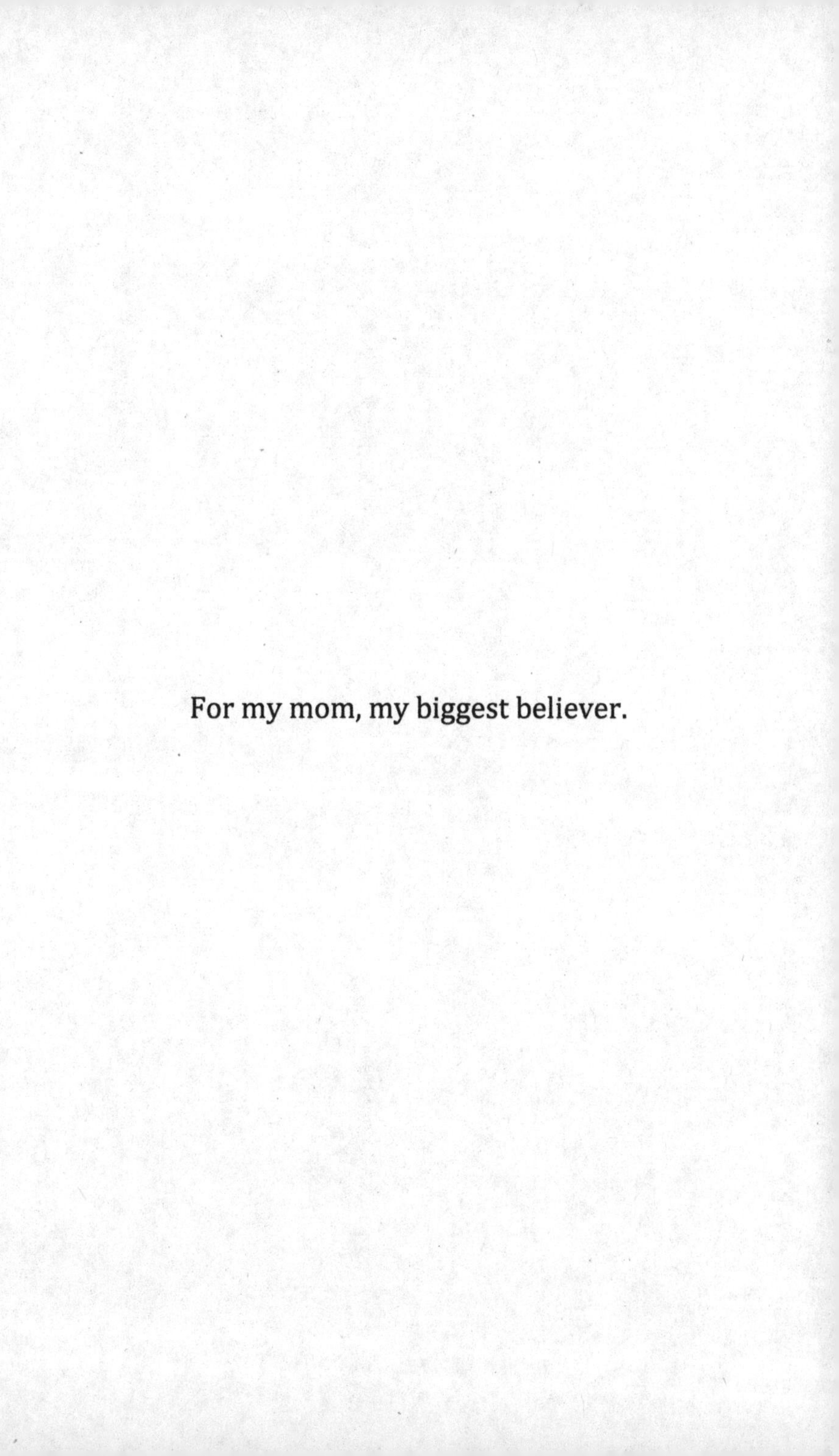

For my mom, my biggest believer.

THE OTHER INSIDE

PART I
HUNGER

CHAPTER 1

The hunger has returned. God knows I have tried to stop, but the need to feed is too great, too persistent. This… this… thing inside of me has taken over. The thing I have come to call the *Other* is my means to survival.

I've kept a good distance from the target, using darkness as cover. Streetlights are now the enemy. Hunting is a painstaking process. It takes skill and patience, both of which are currently being tested. The Other does not know of these virtues. It relies solely on instinct.

The man strolls at an aggravating pace. His head is bowed, his hands shoved deep in the pockets of his yellow jacket. He is probably consumed with thoughts of a warm bed and home-cooked meal, or maybe a late-night fast-food run and a beer. Either way, he does not know he is being followed. He is oblivious to the horror that lurks only twenty feet behind him. Even if he spots me, his eyes would pass over my form with disinterest. To him, I would appear no different than anyone else, at least not initially. His limited scope of imagination would have him thinking I am after some lesser goal, like a wristwatch or wallet. A material threat, not a mortal danger.

The man turns onto Bliss Street Terrace favoring the sidewalk paralleling the woods. The situation has turned in my favor. I slip into the foliage using the thick evergreens as camouflage.

I have been matching his pace until now. I close the gap, dodging branches, and skirting rocks. The dead leaves left over from fall crunch under my weight. The sound is well controlled. I have learned how to blend in with the trees, ensuring the noises I emit mimic the forest. With each step, the man's yellow jacket inches closer. The time for planning is over. I remind the Other this needs to be done quietly. Quickly.

Focus, I caution. The yellow jacket is just a few feet in front of me.

This is it.

Adrenaline rushes through my body in warm waves. The Other takes control. I watch as my fingers close around the man's collar and yank him back into the woods. He lets out a single cry before I can clamp a firm hand over his mouth. Allowing that yelp was sloppy.

My heart slams against my breastbone. "I'm sorry," I say, right before the Other snaps his neck. Removing the box cutter from the back pocket of my jeans, I slash his throat. A rush of hydrating liquid spews forth. Crouching over his lifeless body, the Other feeds.

CHAPTER 2

I wake with a start, my thighs slamming into the underside of the steering wheel. Dammit! I rub my soon-to-be-bruised legs and reflect on why I have been jolted from a deep sleep. It's the regret, I suppose, the irrepressible feeling that I have done something wrong and unnatural.

The sunlight pouring through the windshield is blinding. I feel like shit but, then again, a good night's sleep is hard to come by crammed between a faux leather seat and steering wheel. I reach for the door handle, escaping into the crisp morning air. The trees are a healthy green. The kind of green that comes from ample rain. The birds are in full swing. Their incessant tweeting sounds as if they are auditioning for a choir, each trying to outdo the other's showmanship. It is a New Hampshire spring on the cusp of summer.

I inhale a gulp of fresh air, attempting to clear my head and conscience. My unfortunate potential to find trouble means *always* thinking ahead. Over the years, I have learned to spot warning signs and create rules.

I will not hurt women.

I will not hurt children.

My longevity depends on playing it smart if I am to continue eluding the state police. In nature, the hunted often becomes the hunter and the predator—prey. I do not want my story to end like that.

As I gaze into the surrounding forest, I hope last night's incident was just a bad dream, but the undeniable evidence is right there on my hands and under my fingernails. Suddenly, I cannot help but feel like I am being watched. Closed in on. Are the police on to me? I listen intently for the sound of sirens approaching in the distance. This is how most days start. It's not just the Law I have been running from. It is the guilt. Alone in my head with only the Other for company, I inevitably end up thinking of her.

My mother.

She represents the last of my humanity. After her death, I ran from my hometown, the yellow wallpaper of my kitchen, the safety of my childhood bedroom, and even my brother. Since then, I have been on the move. I have remained in Barren, New Hampshire longer than I should have stayed anywhere.

I walk to the edge of the thin stream running a few feet from my parked car and study the face reflected up at me. It is the face of a broken man. A man that has witnessed too much awfulness and pain. I do not see a young man on the edge of thirty, youth still on his side. I see only sadness behind his green eyes and dried blood around his mouth.

I wipe my lips and study the crimson flakes on the back of my hand. Another failure. I have learned that escaping the Other's hunger is impossible. How do you run from something when it is a part of you?

·　　·　　·

In the shower, I take my time rinsing off the sweat that smells of evergreens and death. As I step onto the cold bathroom tiles, a knock sounds at the door.

"Use whatcha got in there now, Billie. I put some fresh towels in your room for next time. Okay, hun?"

"Thanks, Darlene."

Her footfalls pad down the hall and disappear into the kitchen. Darlene is a sweet woman. She took me in without hesitation when her husband brought me home for dinner one evening after my shift at the convenience store. I had applied for a job at Gus's store, Every Penny Counts, after realizing the small reserve of cash I kept in my glove box was dwindling. I had no work history or references, but I must have looked like I could handle the work. After all, I drive an economy car and comb my hair to one side like everyone else. Gus hired me in an instant. I guess finding reliable employees is difficult in a small-town like Barren. Minimum wage jobs seem to be reserved for teenagers in need of summer pocket money, and help is slim to none when school starts back up.

I worked hard for Gus and Darlene. I stocked shelves, carried heavy boxes, and pumped gas like any law-abiding citizen on the straight and narrow. One night the old man invited me to dinner at his house behind the convenience store. "He's a good boy and hardworking." I had overheard him say to Darlene when I'd excused myself to use the bathroom. "I don't think he has anywhere to go. No family. No friends."

When I returned, they offered to let me stay in one of the storage closets in the store. It was just big enough to cram a cot and small dresser in. There was a toilet across the hall and, as a bonus, I could use their shower at the house whenever I needed. That was almost two years ago now. I guess having people care gave me just enough of a reason not to pack my bags and run again.

Darlene is at the kitchen table with a *Home and Garden* magazine and a steaming mug of tea in front of her. "Billie," she says, perking up at my entrance. "Kettle's still hot if you'd like some tea. I picked up some more chamomile in town. I know it's your favorite." A strand of silver hair falls from a low bun into her eyes. She tucks it behind her ear.

"You're too good to me."

"Nonsense," she replies, returning her attention to the magazine.

"I'm going to pass on tea this time. I'm late for my shift." The truth: I do not deserve chamomile tea with murder so fresh the scent seems to cling to my skin despite my furious scrubbing in the shower.

"I was hoping you'd sit with me for a few."

"Next time," I promise, bending to plant a kiss on her dark, wrinkled cheek.

"You're a good boy, Billie," she calls after me as I shut the storm door.

If only she knew how wrong she was.

CHAPTER 3

Every Penny Counts is the only convenience store and gas station within a fifteen-mile radius of winding country roads. Barren rests on the edge of the White Mountain National Forest and has a population of just under 3,000. It's a small-town that doesn't have room for big-box supermarkets. If you're looking for that, you need to drive twenty minutes to North Conway. That being said, Every Penny Counts sees a fair amount of foot traffic. Gus stocks all the staples of nutrition along with the blow-your-hard-earned-cash items like alcohol, cigarettes, and lottery tickets.

"Keep an eye on those damn kids, Billie," Gus whispers from the cash register. "They're always tryna steal my cigarettes and beer." I don't need to see his hand to know he is caressing the pistol he keeps under the counter for "just in case" scenarios.

I give him a wink. Gus is convinced that every teenager who has ever stepped foot in his store is a kleptomaniac. I do not finger the teenage boys as a problem. They are still young, more likely to pocket candy bars than run out with a six-pack of beer.

I continue unloading box after box of canned soup and macaroni and cheese. The bell above the door jingles. I look up to see the teenagers leaving, fistfuls of candy in their hands as expected.

I resume my work. Gus begins whistling, and I smile. When I first met Gus, he spoke to me like I was a runaway. *Where do you come from? Are you lost? Where are your parents? Your family?* At twenty-seven, I was too old for those kinds of questions. Regardless, I do not talk about my past. I'm not sure what he eventually decided my life's story was. Perhaps he thinks I was a hippie living out of my car and trying to travel the world. Perhaps I was a recovering drug addict caught in a spree of bad luck. Either way, he could never imagine the truth.

The bell above the door jingles again, and Gus's whistling halts. "Hey, Jim. How's it going?"

"Not bad, old man. How's the Missus? She better be feeding you good."

"Can't complain none. Not since we have our Billie here helping out."

I glance up and throw a wave at the fat balding man that smiles back. I open a new box packed with pickles and secure my box cutter.

"I'll take a pack of Marlboro Lights," he says, turning back to Gus. He hinges himself across the counter, the top of his butt crack peeking from his khakis. "I'm glad you have someone here to look out for you." The man hooks a thumb back towards me. "Granted everything that's been happening around here."

Gus furrows his already wrinkled brow, the corners of his mouth turning down beneath his gray beard. "What are you blabbing on about now, Jim?"

The bell above the door sounds again. A young woman enters, diverting to the back of the store where the freezers are located.

The balding man's voice drops almost to a whisper. "You haven't heard about the lunatic cutting people's throats and leaving them in the woods?"

My heart leaps. I edge closer to the man, pretending to busy myself at one of the shelves. Surely, I must have misheard him.

"The most recent one makes four bodies in counting. Each were found in the woods only a few miles from those fancy condominiums. You know, the new ones by the town line?"

Gus nods.

"The police issued a warning this afternoon over the radio. They want people to avoid being outside after dark, and they're warning folks to be on the lookout for anyone suspicious. If you spot something, just dial 911, no hero stuff."

"Jeez. They think all four were murdered by the same person?"

"That's the rumor."

"What about an animal? Maybe a bear? It's getting to be that time of year now."

"Not likely if what they're saying about the bodies is true. I heard all four people had their necks snapped and their throats cut with some type of blade. I don't know many bears that carry a knife around. Do you?"

"Guess not," Gus says.

"Whoever this guy is, he's one sick bastard."

"Sounds like it," Gus replies. "So much for the animal attack idea."

"Things like this aren't supposed to happen in a little town like Barren. The last big death I remember around here was back in '89 when Mrs. O'Neil fell into that well. And she wasn't murdered either. She just goddamn tripped. Probably had one too many whiskeys." Jim scoffs.

"If you ask me, it probably has something to do with those new condominiums. They bring in a lot of city folk looking to experience country life. When outsiders arrive, trouble often comes with 'em."

The woman customer had grabbed a few frozen meals and approaches the register. The balding man glances back at her. "Anyway, Gus, I've got to run. It'll all be in the paper tomorrow morning. Check it out for yourself." He squirrels away the pack of cigarettes in his pant pocket and heads for the door. "Be safe and stay away from those damn condos," he calls as the bell above the door chimes.

. . .

"Billie. Hey, Billie." Gus waves his palm in front of my face.

My eyes bounce around the store. The woman had left. Jim is long gone. It is just the two of us.

"Jesus, boy. Where were you? Space? I'm not paying you to be Buzz fuckin' Aldrin."

"Sorry," I mumble. I bend down, lifting the half-unpacked box of pickles.

"You hear any of that?" he asks.

I nod, desperate to clear the stars that swarm my vision. Bodies found. Throats cut. Police on the lookout. My hands tremble, rattling the glass jars.

"Can you believe the world these days? The people in it? That's some real sick shit."

My mouth is too dry to form words. I hear my pulse drumming in my ears.

"Would you mind if I leave a few minutes early? I'm going to tell Darlene the bad news."

"You'll scare her," I blurt, my pulse quickening. The box of pickle jars nearly topples from my arms.

"Maybe so, but she'll find out eventually. Most likely in tomorrow's paper. My Darlene's a tough cookie. Men are always trying to shield women from the world's pain. If you ask me, imagined horrors are always worse than the real thing."

"Not always," I reply. Heat rushes to my face like I have been caught in a lie. I set the box down and remove the box cutter from my back pocket. I finger the trigger and the blade releases. It is covered in a thick red liquid. My vision tunnels, and the box cutter clatters to the ground.

Gus stoops to retrieve it. I intercept, snatching the box cutter up in a clumsy motion. I begin to stutter, summoning an impossible excuse as to why the box cutter is covered in blood. If only I could think of a way to make Gus understand why I am holding a murder weapon. I glance down. The blade is clean.

"You okay, son?" Gus asks.

I nod.

He returns the gesture, but his expression registers lingering concern. "All right then, make sure you lock up out back," he says as he snatches his keys from the counter and swings open the front door. The bell gives off its final chime of the night.

CHAPTER 4

Seventeen Years Ago

"Your mother's a whore, Billie."

Bill buried his face into the plaid sofa right between the old coffee stain and new cigarette burn. *Whore this, whore that.* Bill heard this statement at least once a day from Frank. He didn't know much about evil stepmothers, those princess stories were for girls, but he knew a thing or two about evil stepfathers—the kind that used their fists instead of words, punctuating each point with a pounding.

Frank paced the hallway of their 1970's bungalow, beer from the can he clenched in one hand sloshing to the floor. The mess didn't matter much. Bill's mother tried to keep the place neat, but it only went so far against a backdrop of stains, dented walls, and outdated appliances atop an old linoleum floor. Bill guessed what they said was true, you can't polish a turd.

"Your mother's a whore," Frank bellowed.

Bill bit his tongue. He wanted to watch television. It was summer vacation after all, a short reprieve before he started middle school in fall. But T.V. was off-limits. Frank did not allow it while he was fighting with Bill's mother who had now locked herself in the bathroom. God forbid the television drown out the yelling, crying, and the sickening sound of fists against flesh.

It was now 4:15 p.m. *Teenage Mutant Ninja Turtles* was on, and he was officially missing it. This was the third missed episode in a row because of his mother and stepfather's domestic disputes. What would he even talk about when school started back up? The kids would mock him, call him a loser. He was tempted to press the power button on the remote. What was the worst thing that could happen? Frank directed his rage towards him instead of his mother. Would that be so bad?

He wiggled to a seated position. The remote was in the center of the coffee table. His finger hovered above the red button. Despite the temptation, memories of past throbbing bruises stopped him from pushing it.

Frank pounded on the bathroom door. The cheap plywood bounced with each hit, threatening to cave in. There were already holes marking the door, indicative of past assaults like notches on a bedpost. "Come out of there, Eve!"

"Just leave me alone."

His mother's response came in a shrilled sob. It was her first words since retreating into the bathroom more than fifteen minutes ago. She had barreled down the hall, Frank hot on her trail, and locked herself behind the safety of the plywood door. It was a scene that was played out often. When she hid in there, Bill feared she would never come out, or *could* never come out. Resolution was not a word in his stepfather's vocabulary.

Bill wished his brother, Fred was home. But Fred was six years older than him, almost eighteen now. He kept his distance by staying out late with friends. Bill squeezed his eyes shut, trying to imagine what his brother would do. He summoned his courage and pushed himself off the sofa. "Mom?"

"Pipe down, Billie," Frank shouted, resuming his incessant banging. "Open this door, Eve, or I swear to God, I'll break it down."

"You aren't the God-fearing type," she called back.

Frank snorted, his beer belly hitching. "You're testing me, woman. Open this door."

"Mom, are you okay?" Bill squeaked.

"Get out here and tell me what you did. I want to hear the words straight from your slut mouth," Frank demanded, drowning out Bill's meek call.

"I didn't do anything!"

"You're gonna tell me you don't have a thing going with Bob, that peon at the Post Office? Huh?"

"No, I—"

"Really? Then how come he keeps calling here and leaving messages on the machine asking for you?"

"I don't know. I... I... must have a package." She was crying again.

"He says he needs you to come down there. I bet I can guess what he wants you down there for."

"It's just a package, Frank. I probably need to sign for it in person."

"I want him to stop calling here."

"That's his job. His job is to call me when I have a package to pick up. This is ridiculous."

"It is *ridiculous*, I know. Ridiculous that I married a good for nothing whore!"

"Mom!" Bill wailed.

Frank spun towards him, his face a bright angry red. "I told you to keep quiet, boy. No one in this house respects me. Did you hear that, Eve? Now I'm gonna have to teach this son of yours some damn respect."

Bill shrunk back as Frank advanced. His stepfather was fast for his size. He seized Bill by the collar hoisting him in the air.

"I'm sorry, Frank," Bill stuttered. "I didn't mean to—"

The bathroom door swung open. It collided with the back wall puncturing the plaster. "Get your hands off of him," Eve challenged.

Suddenly Bill was soaring through the air. He cried out as his lower back connected with the wall on descent. It took him a moment to clear the stars flashing before his eyes. His vision was hazy, but he could make out his mother's slender frame. She was standing her ground, hands clenched by her sides, facing the man she chose to marry after the first two men in her life had left her with two kids.

"Rose petals," she said to Billie.

Bill tried to nod. *Rose petals* was their secret word. A couple of years ago, when Bill was still young, his mother sat with him in his room after a particularly nasty altercation with Frank had left her with a black eye. Bill told her he was scared, that he didn't like it when his stepdad hollered and grabbed her, that he was going to run away. His mother held him until he stopped crying, then asked if he thought roses were pretty. Bill had nodded. "Well, from now on whenever I say *rose petals,* that means I'm okay," she said. "And I want you to think of nice, pretty things like roses instead of running away. I don't know about you, but I can't think of a more beautiful flower than a rose." Bill had agreed. From that moment on, rose petals was *their* word. No one else in the whole world knew what it meant, certainly not Frank.

"Rose petals," his mother mouthed again as Frank seized her by the wrists and dragged her into the kitchen.

Bill squeezed his eyes shut and clamped his hands over his ears. There was no point in listening to the screams he couldn't stop. All he could do was try to think of nice, pretty things like his mother had told him to do. Perhaps she should have told him a secret code word for *I've had enough.*

CHAPTER 5

Scraping and clanging from the store wakes me. My back aches from the rigid cot, but anything beats the Toyota. Sleeping in the car is reserved for desperate nights. Nights when I am too ashamed to return to my room in the convenience store, not wanting to bring filth into a place gifted to me by people who represent the only kindness I have known in a long while. Fragments of lingering nightmares are replaced by thoughts of yesterday's news: the nut case slashing peoples' throats. I launch out of bed. The cot creaks and quivers. I gather my clothes and dress, slipping the box cutter into my back pocket like I always do.

In the store, I find Gus dragging a crate of beer across the wooden floor. The glass bottles clank with each tug.

"Woah, woah. Let me get that," I say, edging him out of the way. I lift the heavy crate and place it by the cooler where I begin unloading it.

"Show off," Gus grunts.

I smirk.

"You're not on the clock for another couple of hours. Don't waste your morning on me."

"It's no problem," I reply. Since the last hunt, my body has been given new strength and energy. The invigoration is like a drug though. In a couple of months, it will wear off.

After that, I'll be right back to weak, sick, dying Billie. In the meantime, I'll buy time by eating food, preferably rare meat. It seems to have a sustaining effect, although not as potent and satisfying as the real thing. Lately, anything else makes me throw up. If Darlene and Gus have noticed my abstinence from vegetables or bread, they haven't said anything.

I load the last beer into the cooler. "Anything else I can do for you, old man?"

"What did I just tell you, kid. Get outta here and enjoy your morning. Maybe head over to the house and have coffee with my beautiful wife."

"I might just do that," I say as I snag the morning newspaper from the rack by the register.

• • •

The newspaper is hot in my clenched hand. Instead of coffee with Darlene, I make the five-minute walk to my car nestled in the trees behind Gus's property. I rest my back against the Toyota's hood and unfold the paper. **Murder in a Sleepy Town** is printed on the front page in bold accusing text. My jaw clenches as I skim the article:

The hour was late when Barren resident, Michael Tremont, began his nightly walk. Little did he know this harmless ritual would end in devastation. On May 25th, police discovered Michael's body after an eight-hour search in the forest surrounding the Bliss Street Terrace Condominiums, two miles from the victim's home.

"The body wasn't hard to spot. The assailant did little to conceal it, and the victim had been wearing a bright yellow jacket," explained Arthur Crispen, town sheriff.

Police believe Michael's murder is linked to at least three other homicides spanning the Barren and North Conway area. "Attacks have all happened at night. Victims have been male, between the ages of twenty-five and forty-nine. We are still looking for a connection between these men." Crispen refused to comment further, assuring the public will be made aware as new developments unfold.

Law enforcement is cautioning residents to limit time outside after dark. Barren residents are horrified by these recent murders and are all asking the same question: how does something like this happen in a sleepy town?

I crumble the paper into a tight ball and whip it at the ground. The article's question enrages me, sending my heart into a hectic rhythm, igniting the Other inside. Are the residents of this town really that naive?

These small towns are all the same. I've blown through a handful of them leaving just before they figure it out. Luckily, small-town law enforcement is not used to dealing with violent crime. They barely know a moving violation from a parking ticket. They readily accepted my cover-ups: a rash suicide, a rare hunting incident, a freak fishing accident. They believed what they wanted to believe. What I made them believe.

Small-town people think they can leave their keys in their ignitions, their doors unlocked at night, their windows cracked to let in the cool breeze. They don't worry about the consequences. They don't realize they are tempting the Other. They do not understand that it must feed on them. I don't want to do it. God, I don't. But I am compelled to take their lives to save my own. It's what the Other demands. There is no asking or negotiating. I have tried that already.

These things happen in a sleepy town precisely because everyone *is* asleep. Nobody is paying attention until it's too late. Until I have already come and gone.

"Wake up," I scream into the woods. "Wake up!"

CHAPTER 6

Seventeen Years Ago

His mother had a swollen lip again. Frank usually avoided her face so people wouldn't ask questions. Occasionally he slipped up though, leaving her with a black eye or bruised cheek.

Her lip was bad, the left corner an irritated, puffy pink. Bill studied the injury as she lay next to him in his bed, one hand cradling her head. Her long, dark hair grazed the quilt giving off the faint scent of cigarettes and perfume. Even with the swollen lip, she looked beautiful. She'd tell you otherwise, of course, but Bill paid her no mind. He suspected every son found their mother beautiful in their own way. After all, a mother was the first woman you fell in love with.

"Why does he do it?" Bill asked, his fingers closing around his dinosaur print sheets. Too bad the sheets weren't Frank's throat. Bill wanted to hurt him the way he hurt his mother.

His mother sighed. "Some people have darkness in them, Billie. Sometimes they can hide it. Other times, it slips out like with Frank."

"Well, maybe he should try to hide it better then." Bill's tone was curt, insensitive. His mother didn't deserve his anger too. He knew that but, for some reason, he couldn't help it. Their marriage, the violence, it was frustrating and scary.

"He wasn't always like this," his mother said. "The drinking, it didn't really start until after Frank hurt his back at the lumber yard. He can't work anymore because of it. He's in pain. Sometimes when people don't work their days are too long, too empty, and they get themselves into trouble." She paused. "He used to be a good man."

"Frank's an asshole," Bill said bluntly. The swear rolled off his tongue with ease, as if he had decades of experience identifying *assholes* not just his short twelve years.

"Frank is my husband," she responded.

"But he's not my dad."

"No," she said. "He's not. But he's all you have."

Bill felt his face flush with anger. "I've got Freddy."

"Fred is a good brother, isn't he?"

Bill thought of all the times his brother had covered his skinned knees with bandages or slung an arm around him while they were held up in Fred's room as their mother and stepfather argued.

"I'm glad you have each other," his mother said. "After me and Fred's father divorced, I didn't think I would have any more children."

"Until you met my dad?" Bill asked. His heart fluttered with anticipation. He had always known that he and Fred were half-brothers. It didn't bother either of them. They both grew up without their real dads. As far as they were concerned, they had no fathers just their mother. But, as a rule, his mother never talked about their fathers much, especially Billie's. He wondered what she would say this time. How much he could get out of her.

His mother nodded. "That's right, until I met your dad."

"Where?" Bill asked.

She shook her head and smiled. "Oh, Billie."

Bill's stomach dropped. She was brushing him off again. He prayed silently that she would answer. "Come on, Mom. Where?"

She rolled her brown eyes. "You really want to know?"

Of course, he wanted to scream. *Of course, I want to know about my real dad!* He nodded.

"All right," she said, pausing to brush his hair back with her palm. "It was a crazy time here in our little town. All these animals, some of them pets, were turning up dead. Not from natural causes either, more like animal attacks. Eventually, a rumor went around that a person was doing it. Some deranged psychopath who combed the woods in search of their next kill. People became wary of strangers passing through. One night, when I was working at the bar, this out-of-towner drifted in. He minded his own business, just came in for a beer, but people didn't like that much. They stared and snickered. I felt bad, so I spent the night talking to him." She smiled at the memory.

"He had these beautiful green eyes, just like yours," she said, bopping him on the nose. "I don't know. There was just something about him I liked, something special. I thought… well, it doesn't matter what I thought would happen. What I did was make a mistake. I invited him to spend the night at my house. In the morning, he was gone. Poof. Like he'd never even existed. The next day, I got a few judgmental stares from some folks at the bar who didn't like me fraternizing with an outsider, but soon things settled down. The animal killings stopped. People relaxed. Little did I know that I was carrying a little you inside me."

"He just left?" Bill asked.

"Hmm-mmm. Men do that sometimes. Women too, I suppose. But your dad had no way of knowing that he left you behind though."

Bill had so many questions, perhaps more now than he did before. "What was he like? Was he nice?"

"Oh, honey, I don't know. I barely knew him. Your mom doesn't normally do *things* like that with people she doesn't know. There was just something special about him. Different. From what little I gathered; I'd say he was nice though." The corners of her mouth upturned, her swollen lip growing even larger. "Now, enough of that. You, young man, need to go to bed." She stood. "Did you brush those choppers?"

Bill nodded.

"Good," she said, tucking him in. She planted a kiss on his forehead. "Love you."

"I love you too, Mom."

He watched his mother retreat to the bedroom door with thoughts of his mysterious father consuming his mind. Bill had green eyes just like him, she'd said. How else did he take after his father? He marveled at the idea of sharing DNA with someone he didn't even know and would probably never meet.

His mother switched off the light, pausing in the doorway. "Rose petals," she said and shut the door.

CHAPTER 7

It has been just over two weeks since law enforcement issued the warning. They have yet to release further information regarding the homicides. I check the newspaper religiously. Few articles have been published since then. Some report police have a suspect in custody. Others deny this, claiming it is only a matter of time until the killer strikes again. Fear sells. Lack of press, however, leads me to believe everyone is hoping it all just goes away.

One journalist reported saliva was found around the wounds on the victims' throats. With no confirmation from law enforcement, that piece was quickly shot down as rumor.

Barren hasn't forgotten, but it has relaxed as sleepy towns often do. Without another murder, people are gradually staying out later. They allow their children to play outside and their pets to roam free. Without the constant reminder from the press, it is easy for them to forget. The media has a god-like ability to control people. They can create terror, elicit panic, or ensue calm based solely on what they print. And the public listens. They take each article as Gospel as if God himself came down from the heavens and took a part-time job at the New York Times. But even the press has moved on. There are bigger stories, scarier stories. Gang violence persists in Detroit. A father throws himself in front of a train in Boston. And no one is quite sure what the President will do next.

Of course, police assure us they are still in pursuit of the killer. Yet if they were really being honest, they would admit they too have little to go on. They have no witnesses. The DNA collected from the victims will reveal no matches in the system. The crime scenes have yet to be discovered because all the bodies had been moved to a secondary location.

As for me, I feel myself becoming weaker with each passing day. I know it is only a matter of time until the Other makes an appearance, and I am forced to hunt again. Hunger lurks in the depth of my stomach. With each grumble, the Other threatens to emerge early from its hibernation. I remain calm only because the police have no suspects or at least no *real* suspects. They are reaching like they always do when there is no one obvious to blame. They target local petty criminals, the sex offenders, or the weird guy that every neighborhood seems to have living in his mother's basement.

"What are your plans for today?" Darlene asks, cutting through my thoughts like a knife.

I finish chewing the bacon I'd shoved into my mouth in an attempt to satisfy my hunger. I wish it was raw. Slimy. Bloody. I think of the man in the yellow jacket. I hear the snap his neck had made when it broke. I see the silver gleam of the blade as it slashed, followed by the rush of hydrating blood. "Don't know. Might go for a drive," I say.

"Where about?" Gus asks in between a mouthful of scrambled eggs. I can tell he is anxious to get to the store, but as a ritual, every Saturday Darlene makes him open late so they can enjoy a proper family breakfast.

I shrug. "Haven't decided yet." I stare at my plate. The bacon is gone. I still have a small pile of eggs to force down my gullet.

"Billie's a free spirit," Darlene remarks.

I take a forkful of scrambled eggs and stuff them in my mouth. I swallow the yellow mush like a pill, suppressing a grimace as it slides down my esophagus.

"So, Mr. Free Spirit, what do you do on these drives of yours?" Gus asks.

"Depends. Sometimes I go somewhere to hike. Other times I find a place to sit down with a beer." *Or, I stalk my next victim with the Other's demands ringing in my ears*, I think.

"Well, that sounds wonderful," Darlene gushes. "Maybe you will meet a nice girl on one of these trips. You sure are handsome enough."

"Yeah, get yourself a girl tonight, Billie." Gus winks at me.

I feel the heat of a blush spread across my cheeks. Sometimes Gus and Darlene really are like my parents. They never had any children of their own. Darlene is African American and Gus some mix of European. From what they've told me, their parents did not approve of their marriage. It got ugly between the two families quick, and a ridiculous prejudice kept them from fulfilling their dreams of having children. Now, in their early seventies, it is too late to try. I think having me around allows them to imagine what it would have been like if they'd had kids. It seems they want nothing more than for me to meet somebody and settle down. Maybe have a few rascals who someday may even refer to them as Grandma and Grandpa. But how am I supposed to raise a family while making minimum wage and living in a storage closet is another question? More importantly, having a family is something the Other would never permit.

I push back from the table, gathering my plate and coffee mug. "Thank you for breakfast, Darlene. I'm going to shower then head out. Probably be back late."

"Oh, Billie." Darlene stands. "Please be careful tonight. They still haven't caught that… that…"

"Lunatic," Gus interjects.

Darlene nods.

"Don't worry about me," I say. "I can take care of myself."

CHAPTER 8

Fifteen Years Ago

Bill was in his bedroom reading comics when the doorbell rang. He listened to Frank's angry grunts as he hoisted himself out of the tattered armchair stationed in front of the television.

"Get down here, Billie," Frank shouted. "It's Clarice."

At the mention of her name, Bill tossed aside *The Adventures of Spiderman* and bolted downstairs. She was standing on the front porch, her silky, brunette hair pulled back into a neat ponytail. She wore a pale blue tank top that showed off her tanned skin and budding breasts.

"Hey, Billie," she said. "Want to hang out?"

Bill glanced at Frank for approval and realized his stepfather was also staring at her chest. Frank smirked. "You're getting to be a big girl, honey. What are you sixteen now?"

"We are fourteen," Bill grunted, pushing past his stepfather onto the porch. "Come on," Bill urged, taking her hand.

"Frank's an asshole. I wish my mom would just leave him already," Bill said. They were seated in the tall grass under the big oak tree in his backyard. They had wasted the last few precious weeks of their summer vacation trying to get to the top of that damn tree. But the old oak was ancient. The twisted, entangled branches made the climb treacherous.

"At least your mom's nice. My mom is a total control freak," Clarice said, glancing over her shoulder towards the direction of her house. She lived a few houses down but, because of the large property sizes, it was about a ten-minute walk. "And my dad… well… it's nothing."

"What's wrong with your dad?"

Clarice stared at the grass while twirling a thin blade around her finger. "It's nothing really. He just always thinks I'm lying about things when I'm not. Like if I get sick, he thinks I'm faking it. If I tell him I finished my homework, he says I'm just trying to get out of doing it. My mom told me once he was furious that I'd been a girl. And, unfortunately, they never had any more kids, so I'm all he's got."

"I didn't know your dad was like that. I always thought he was, well, kind of cool."

"Yeah, real cool," Clarice murmured. "He probably likes you because you're a guy."

"Parents shouldn't do that. They shouldn't be angry with you for something you have no control of." Like Frank being angry that Bill was ever born for instance. If Bill knew the shit he'd have to put up with when his mother married his stepfather, he would've thought twice about coming into the world.

"Parents suck," Clarice sighed.

Despite what Clarice said, Bill liked her parents, especially her mom. She brought them carrot sticks and fresh fruit when they were playing. Sometimes she made them homemade lemonade or hot chocolate when it was cold. Their house was clean, and there was never any yelling, not like at his house anyway. Clarice's dad even let them watch HBO movies and stay up late. It was how Bill saw *The Exorcist* for the first time: huddled beneath a blanket, Clarice snuggled by his side, a bowl of popcorn between them. Her grandmother lived with them too. She was a vivacious woman filled with wisecracks and opinions. She allowed them to call her by her first name, June. June passed on tidbits of advice whenever she saw fit. Like the time she told Billie breasts weren't made for breastfeeding, they were made for looking good in a sweater.

On the other side of the spectrum, there was *his* family. Bill's mom did the best she could. He knew that deep down. She worked nights at the bar and slept most of the day. They didn't have a lot of money. They didn't have carrot sticks or fresh fruit, and they certainly didn't have homemade lemonade. All that he could forgive. It was her decision to stay married to Frank that he could not. He had begged her countless times to leave him, but she always refused. "I'm getting old, Billie. I'd be lonely. Besides, Frank takes care of us," she said. Bill couldn't wrap his mind around her outlook on their marriage. Did Frank take care of them by sitting on the couch all day collecting disability from an accident at the lumber yard that happened almost ten years ago? Did he take care of them by calling him names and pushing his mother around? Bill thought not. And as soon as he turned eighteen, he was out of there, and he'd take his mother with him.

"What do you think high school will be like?" Clarice asked, interrupting his thoughts.

"Probably more of the same," he responded. Starting high school this fall was an endeavor Bill was not looking forward to.

"At least we'll have each other," she said. Someone had to be optimistic.

"Dinner's ready," Frank hollered from the doorway. "Get your ass inside, boy."

Clarice rolled her eyes. "Ugh, he is horrible."

They both giggled.

Frank peered across the yard, rubbing his fat gut. "Your mother says Clarice is welcome to stay too," Frank said, then disappeared into the house.

. . .

Bill's mother was not known for her cooking. Most nights it was T.V. dinners in front of the television while trying to stay out of Frank's way. Tonight, there was a feast of mashed potatoes, steak, and steamed broccoli, probably from a bag but at least it was green. They even sat at the kitchen table perhaps assuming the appearance of a normal family for Bill's brother who was there too. Fred moved out a few months back and visited seldom. Bill didn't blame him. Frank was a piece of shit who had a way of making people feel unwelcome.

At the table, they participated in forced conversation when his mother opened with, "Are you two excited for high school?"

Clarice smiled and nodded whereas each question gave Bill more anxiety. *Do you guys have any classes together? Do you know any of the teachers? Do you think you'll go to homecoming?*

"A pretty girl like you, Clarice, will have the boys lined up to take you to homecoming," Frank interjected, licking gravy from his fingers.

Clarice smiled, a blush turning her face a rosy pink. "Thanks, Mr. Dunne."

Bill suppressed a grimace. Mr. Dunne was too formal of a title for his stepfather. Mr. Dunne should be reserved for the dad that tosses the football around the backyard with his son.

"If you're lucky, maybe she'll even take someone worthless like you, Billie." Frank laughed at this, sending spittle into the air. He batted the top of Billie's head. A gesture that appeared playful, but Frank always did things just a little too hard.

"Screw you," Bill mumbled, smoothing his brown locks flat.

"What did you say, boy?" Frank demanded.

"Homecoming is lame anyway," Fred commented over Frank's grumbles. "Overrated if you ask me. You kids will have plenty of time before prom to figure the whole high school thing out." He winked across the table at Bill.

"Anyone want something to drink?" His mother chimed in. "Freddy?"

"Freddy and Billie. Names for a bunch of pansies," Frank muttered.

"What was that, dear? Would you like a beverage?" Eve asked.

Frank grunted and returned his attention to his plate, stabbing at his steak with a fork.

"I'd love to go to homecoming with you, Billie," Clarice said.

Fred gave Bill's leg a quick kick under the table. The brother's locked eyes and grinned.

After dinner, Bill's mother offered for Frank to escort Clarice home. She agreed and began putting on her shoes.

"Come on, missy. I'll drive. It will be faster," Frank said.

Clarice eyed the beer can in his hand.

"It's only right down the street," he scoffed.

She hesitated but went with him anyway.

Bill watched them leave from the window before joining Fred on the couch to play Nintendo. Almost an hour later, Frank returned from a trip that should have only taken a few minutes, explaining he stopped at the liquor store for more booze. Bill glared at him.

"What are you looking at you little shit," Frank slurred from the doorway. He snorted and traveled down the hall with a fresh beer.

CHAPTER 9

I decide to drive into the city where I like to people-watch. Gas is expensive, so the two-hour drive to Concord happens rarely. No matter where I park, somehow, I always end up in the same park on the same bench with green grass surrounding me and the scent of dahlias filling my nostrils.

The sun is setting. Most people are off work and are out enjoying what remains of the day. Couples lounge in the park, sprawled upon blankets sharing late lunches and books. A group of men play Frisbee to my left. A woman walks by with her golden retriever. The dog stops in front of me to thoroughly sniff around my foot. The retriever growls. The owner apologizes. The two continue, the woman dragging her angry dog behind her as he holds my gaze. He must have sensed the Other.

As the sun disappears, people vacate the park. I am invisible to them as they pass. Thoughts of dinner, last-minute errands, and tomorrow's endeavors are on their minds.

The real pleasure of people-watching is imagining what it is like to be them. A normal person with a normal job who is on their way home to their normal house in a pleasantly normal neighborhood. Are they returning home to their husbands or wives? Will they receive a sloppy lick from their dog instead of a hateful growl? These fantasies of mine are a sweeping overgeneralization of course, but I cannot help but think these people do not live the same life as me. A life filled with blood, desperation, and shame.

Soft gurgles emanate from my abdomen. A stomach on the edge of hunger. The bacon from earlier did little to suppress it. In the past, I have been able to go four, sometimes six months before needing to feed again. I worry. It has only been two weeks.

It is something I should be able to stop but, when a craving hits, there seems to be little I can do to prevent the Other from poking its ravenous head. I am like an alcoholic that is drinking themselves to death. With each sip, their liver is one step closer to shutting down. Their family and friends scream, "Why are you doing this to yourself? Why can't you just stop?" But what only the alcoholic and I understand is, it's not that simple to *just* stop. In fact, sometimes we would rather die than stop.

When it is time to feed, I should hunt outside of Barren. Maybe I will even travel as far as Vermont or New York. If the newspaper articles speak any truth, the police are still on high alert. Part of me believes people-watching will provide a cure. That's why I started doing it in the first place, with the hope that seeing innocent people interact with the world would instill some mercy in my animalistic heart. Some might think it foolish. Some might even think it sick to sit and observe the creatures one feeds on. But is it really any different than people visiting farms? After all, those happy cows in green pastures are the same cows drained of their blood, ground up, and slapped on a hamburger bun with some ketchup and a side of fries.

Another gurgle from my gut. I resume my watching, ignoring it. Two women approach, a blonde and brunette.

They are dressed in black from head to toe. Variants of entwined crosses and ribbons dangle from their throats. The blonde's outfit is more intense: spiked heels, black lipstick, pointed nails. But there is something so familiar about the brunette. We lock eyes and, instantly, I realize who she is. She was my neighbor growing up. My long-lost best friend, Clarice. My heart accelerates as I brace myself to stand. She brushes by, her blue eyes drifting over me like I am just another stranger.

The moment is gone.

It is obvious now that I should have made a move. Of course she didn't recognize me. It's been almost eleven years. Why hadn't I called her name? There are so many things I want to ask her.

So, I stand and follow them.

• • •

Clarice and the blonde pause outside a place called The Den. They flash their ID's at the bouncer before disappearing inside. From the neon sign and pounding bass, I gather The Den is a night club. I start forward then reconsider. I don't belong in places like this. I look around. There is no line out front. Only a few people are propped against the building smoking or vaping, each dressed exactly how Clarice and the blonde had been. I glance down at my own attire of worn jeans, old work boots, and a green T-shirt. It will have to do.

I march forward slipping my wallet from my back pocket, praying my ID isn't expired. The bouncer takes a quick peek then gives me a once-over. He raises an eyebrow. "You sure you're at the right place?"

I nod, but my heart flip-flops. What did he mean by that? What does he see when he looks at me? Does he see a monster? Does he know I'm the guy the police are searching for only a few towns over? For a moment, I panic. Is there blood smeared across my lips? Is my body covered with dirt and the scent of the woods? I brace myself, waiting for him to pull me aside while someone dials 911.

"All right," he says. "Go on in. We don't discriminate here."

As I enter, I read the sign posted in the entryway: *Welcome to Goth Night.* Followed by either the club's motto or a bad play on a Nirvana song: *Come as you are, or as you were.*

CHAPTER 10

The door swings open, and I am greeted by neon brilliance. Hues of pink, purple, and blue flash upon the club's interior. The pounding of electronic bass drums through the soles of my feet. Another flash of color provides a glimpse of the entangled sweaty bodies moving to the music: gyrating, jumping, fists pounding into the air. I divert to the bar.

I order a gin and tonic as a thick bead of sweat slides down my temple. It must be ninety degrees in here. I sip the drink gratefully and turn to survey the crowd. I spot *her* instantly.

She is holding a drink, swaying back and forth to the beat. The blonde leans forward and whispers something in her ear. Clarice throws her head back in laughter, more than half of her drink sloshing to the floor. She glances at her mess, mocks a pout, then breaks into more giggles. I realize I am smiling too as if included in her group, but I'm not and force my lips back into a straight line.

Clarice diverts from her friends. A skinny guy in tight jeans reaches for her hand, urging her backward. He has smooth dark skin and perfectly tousled hair. He has the type of face women like. Clarice shakes him off. She moves for the open spot beside me and rests her forearms on the bar top. She leans forward, probably hoping the bartender will pick her out among the sea of thirsty guests.

I gulp my gin and tonic… this is my chance. It is literally now or never.

"Hi," I stutter, revolted by the insecurity in my voice.

She smiles my way then refocuses on the bartender.

"Are you…" I begin but cannot seem to form words. My mouth goes dry, and I down the rest of my cocktail. "You're Clarice, right?" The gin gives me just enough courage to speak.

Her brow furrows. "Yeah. Do I—"

"It's me, Billie. Billie Dunne. I don't know if you remember—"

"Billie!" Her eyes go wide. "Holy shit! I thought you looked familiar, but I never expected to run into you *here* of all places. You look so different."

She looks different too. A diamond sparkles from her small nose. Her hair is shorter than it had been in high school, hovering just above her shoulders. But what hasn't changed is her eyes. Big pools of sky blue. Eyes that cause you to go weak in the knees if you stare into them for too long.

"It's good to see you, Clarice."

She wrinkles her nose. "Everyone calls me Clare now… I prefer it."

I frown. There is so much I don't know about her.

"Clarice is a bit Hannibal Lectorish, you know?" Her cheeks dimple. We laugh.

"Yeah, I suppose so."

She studies me, perhaps waiting for me to say more. "Can I buy you a drink?" I ask.

• • •

"Come on, Billie," she says while pulling on my arm like an excited child. "Let's find somewhere to catch up."

"I don't want your boyfriend to get mad," I blurt, reminded of the skinny guy with nice hair. The guy who had pulled her back when she'd turned to leave. The last thing I need is an altercation because of some misunderstanding. Things escalate quickly when alcohol and women are involved. If the police were to get called, that could end badly for me.

"My boyfriend?" Her forehead wrinkles. She hooks a thumb back at the skinny guy. "You mean Mason? He is not my boyfriend."

I nod. Women are not my area of expertise, but I know that when a woman says the guy they're with isn't their boyfriend, the guy probably feels differently. And if they really aren't the boyfriend, you can damn well bet they want to be.

"Follow me," she says, her hand still attached to my arm.

So, I give in, allowing her to drag me through the hoard of sweaty dancing bodies. The pounding bass and flashing strobe lights are overwhelming. I squeeze her hand tighter. If I lose her now, I am not sure I will be able to find her again.

We push deeper into the swarm. The drink I attempt to steady in my hand spills to the floor. Glassy eyed drunks step into our path. Someone even slaps my ass as we pass by. Sweat pours down my face. We might never get out of this mash of drunk people. Then, I see an opening. The light at the end of the tunnel, or more accurately, the word 'Lounge' illuminated in incandescent red. Clare leads me to an empty booth in a corner where the music is quieter. I slide into the seat across from her and sip what meager portion remains of my cocktail.

"It's insane in here tonight," Clare says.

"Tell me about it."

We proceed to talk our way through each other's lives, asking and answering all the questions people have after not seeing each other for eleven years. *Where do you live? What do you do for work? Do you remember so-and-so?*

I learn Clare attended the University of New Hampshire and majored in English. She works at a small publishing house specializing in nonfiction books. It's not the best job, but it pays the bills. Writing and reading poetry are her secret pleasures. She had a serious relationship for three years before they split. He wanted kids; she wasn't ready.

The questions prove increasingly more difficult for me. My life is significantly less interesting and the secrets much greater than poetry. Lies threaten to form on my tongue, but honesty is usually better. When you are honest, you don't need to worry about forgetting the lies later. So, I tell her about my gig stocking shelves at the convenience store. I share a few funny stories about Gus and Darlene. I say I have a tiny apartment which is not entirely a lie. I just fail to mention my apartment is a closet with a cot and dresser.

"How are your parents?" I ask.

"They're good. To be honest, they haven't changed much in the past decade. They're still living in the old neighborhood. My dad wants to downsize, but I don't think my mom's ready." She sips her drink. "How about your… I mean… have you been back to visit?"

I take a long swallow of my drink before shaking my head. "I haven't been back in eleven years." The memory surfaces then.

Blood.

There is so much blood.

"Yeah, I understand. Listen, I'm sorry, Billie. I should have never asked." Her gaze falls to the table. "I wasn't sure if you still talked to your brother."

"No, we lost contact," I manage to mumble, but the images are consuming my mind. The deep red pool is expanding. My stepfather kneels before it, a human heap in front of him. He is screaming. God, he is screaming like I have never heard him do before. It is a horrible cry that feels like glass has exploded in my head, shards sticking into my brain. My throat hurts. A bad taste in my mouth. *What has he done?*

"Billie?" Clare places her hand on top of mine.

"Sorry." I recoil from her touch, desperate for my gin and tonic. The remainder of the beverage glides smoothly down my throat. *I don't want to talk about it. I don't even want to think about that day ever again,* is what I want to yell. I let Clare steer the conversation instead. She is smart enough to know that I do not want to talk about my family.

"Remember when we were kids? We were, I don't know, maybe fourteen and we spent all summer trying to climb that damn oak tree in your back yard," she says.

"Ugh, that was horrible. Those branches were so gnarled we could barely get our footing."

She smiles. "No matter how many times we failed, we'd be back out there the next day."

"Isn't that the definition of insanity?"

"What?" She wrinkles her nose. "Doing the same thing over and over and expecting different results?"

I nod.

"Yup. I think you hit the nail on the head. We were both insane. Totally whacked out of our minds."

I chuckle. "I don't think we ever did make it to the top of that tree. Well, I definitely went higher than you, but—"

"Liar," she says, giving me a playful swat.

I smirk.

"We thought those days would last forever," Clare admits, looking down. "I guess we grew up."

I want to object, but it is true. We never did play again. Our dying friendship was not intentional. We just drifted apart. That fall, we started high school. Clare grew her hair long and began wearing makeup. The guys took notice. She evolved into the type of girl that people stopped in the hall to gossip with, that got invited to parties, that skipped school to drive to the beach and drink beers stolen from parents. I, on the other hand, failed to thrive. I was never really bullied, not in the conventional sense anyway. Instead, I was invisible, which sometimes I suspect is worse.

Once in geography, Mr. Tyler called my name, and a girl up front replied, "We don't have a Bill in our class." Mr. Tyler pointed to the back corner where I sat. "Yes, we do. He's right there." The whole class spun around and stared at me like I was an alien the government captured and put on display behind bars.

Clare did not recall that particular incident, and I let her tell the stories for the rest of the night. We are really hitting it off, picking our friendship up almost exactly where we had abandoned it.

"I used to see you peeking through the fence when I'd be out tanning." Clare giggles.

Oh no! Heat rushes up my neck and onto my cheeks. "I… I'm sorry. I don't know why I did that." But I did know why. I simply couldn't help myself. We had been sixteen, and she was beautiful. She would take her bikini top off and lay on her stomach and, if I looked at just the right angle, I could make out the swell of her tanned breasts glistening in the sun.

"It's okay."

"No Clarice—Clare, it's *not* okay. I was young, stupid. I didn't want you to know I did that ever." My hand rises to my forehead, wiping at the fresh sweat beginning to accumulate.

"And I didn't want you to know that I liked it," she says with a mischievous smile.

My jaw nearly falls to the table. If all this time she liked me, how did we manage to drift apart? Why had she gone to homecoming with Brett Cushing instead of me? I want to ask her all these things, but the lights flick on, the music coming to a sudden halt.

Clare glances at her cellphone. "Wow! It's already 1:00 a.m. While I'm thinking of it, let me get your phone number."

"I don't have a cellphone."

"You can't be serious?"

"Call me old fashion."

"Or a loser. All right, well, we will deal with that later. Nightcap at my place? It's right down the street."

I nod and, once again, I follow her.

CHAPTER 11

We are outside on the sidewalk when her friends spot us. People are still filing out of the club, and the pair is forced to zig-zag through the drunken crowd. The blonde approaches with the skinny guy, Clarice had called Mason, in tow.

"Clare, there you are! We wondered where you snuck away to," the blonde gushes, her cheeks a warm pink. "Who's the guy?"

"This is Billie. He is one of my oldest friends." Clare interlaces her arm with mine.

The action is so casual it is like eleven years were never lost between us. I feel a rush of pride course through my veins. My back straightens the tiniest bit. I imagine this is what it would have felt like walking into homecoming with her at my side.

"Hey," the blonde says. "I'm Grace. This is Mason."

Mason steps forward, extending his hand. "Nice to meet you, man."

His forearms are filled with intricate tattoos, and his fingers are adorned with various silver rings. I unhook my arm from Clare's and return the gesture. A small smile plays on Mason's lips, accompanied by the slightest narrowing of his eyes. It is clear he is not happy to meet me; just happy I am no longer attached to Clare.

I fall back to Clare's side consumed by the uncontrollable urge to sling my arm around her waist and pull her close to me. This tattooed nobody could not possibly know Clare the way I do. I knew her back when she was Clarice, before all the dark eyeliner, piercings, and black. But why had she changed the way she looked? Did she do it because she was trying to fit in with Grace and Mason? Maybe I did not know her as well as I thought. Who was I kidding? I didn't even know she preferred to be called Clare now.

"We are going to have a nightcap at my place. You guys in?" Clarice asks.

"Duh," Grace says.

Mason nods.

.   .   .

We walk to Clare's one-bedroom apartment above a pizza place, two blocks from The Den. She claims it is horrible for her diet. The warm scent of garlic and cheese rising through the floorboards gives her horrible cravings. I must admit that even at 1:15 a.m., the scent of pizza still lingers.

The apartment is small and old. Much like her wardrobe, Clare has chosen black as the main color scheme. There are gothic touches to the apartment: dark-colored candles, skulls, a vase of decaying roses. However, there are also signs of life: a bowl stocked with fresh fruit, a reusable water bottle by the sink, her laptop left open on the counter.

We are seated around her coffee table. Grace is sprawled across the armchair. I am on the loveseat by myself. Mason had jumped for the spot next to Clare on the couch. Cards are spread out before us, a game of rummy long abandoned. We had been sidetracked with conversation and booze. I do not drink often, and my head already feels woozy as I crack open another beer.

"Ooh! I have an idea," Grace announces. "Let's play Never Have I Ever!"

"Wow, how original, Grace. Are you sure you don't want to play Truth or Dare while we're at it? Maybe tell ghost stories, make friendship bracelets, and braid each other's hair," Mason mocks.

Clare elbows him. He uses the opportunity to laugh and inch himself closer to her. Their thighs are nearly touching. I gulp down half my beer.

"Truth or Dare isn't a bad idea, Mason, but we all know you're chicken shit," Grace muses. "Anyway, you all know the game. We hold up three fingers and take turns saying things we've *never* done. If you've done it, drop a finger, and take a drink. Easy as that."

"Fine, but let's keep this interesting," Mason says. "Loser takes a shot."

"You're on," Clare challenges.

I smile, doing my best to conceal my growing uneasiness. In my twenty-nine years, I have never played a game like this.

"I'll start," Grace declares. "Never have I ever kissed a girl."

"Come on, Grace. Not fair. That is a deliberate attack," Mason insists while lowering his ring finger, throwing an unintentional peace sign.

I also lower a finger. I may not have played drinking games, but I have been with a woman. We dated for a few months after I left my hometown. Aside from that, there was the brief kiss I shared with Clare when we were teenagers. She must remember that. I look in her direction, but she does not meet my gaze. I take another sip of beer. The bottle is almost empty.

To my surprise, Clare also lowers a finger. "What?" she declares to the room, a blush spreading across her cheeks. "It was college."

"Your turn, Billie," Grace announces.

My heart accelerates. I sip my drink, desperate for their eyes to be off me. What could I say I've never done? Never have I ever taken a life. Nope. Couldn't say that, could I? I take another large swig of beer draining the bottle. *Say something, Billie. Anything.* "Never have I ever… um…" This time, my eyes lock with Clare's. "Gone to college."

All their fingers drop, and they each groan before sipping their drinks.

"That was a good one," Grace says.

"Okay, I've got one," Clare gushes. "Never have I ever tried coffee."

"Shut up!" Grace yells. "There is no way that's true."

"I swear. I've never tried the stuff." She laughs. "I knew I'd get you guys with that. It's my secret weapon."

She was right. Each of our fingers drop. I am forced to crack open another bottle, my buzz dangerously straddling the line of drunk.

Grace huffs. "Kissed a girl, but never tried coffee my ass," she mutters.

"It's official," Mason announces. "I'm going to buy you a coffee tomorrow morning."

"No way. The stuff looks vile, and it's addictive."

"I promise you'll like it." He reaches his arm behind her, letting it rest around her waist.

Clare allows him to leave it there a moment before scooting forward to the edge of the couch. "That's what I'm afraid of." She angles towards him. "Come on, badass. Your turn. Each of us have only one finger left. You have the opportunity to end this right now." She shows him her middle finger.

"Very funny." Mason reclines, scratching his head. "Give me a minute."

It appears Mason is having as difficult of a time as I did. I steal another quick drink from my beverage. The room sways. I haven't had a buzz like this in years. It is kind of fun, allowing me a glimpse into the normal lives of young adults. I peer around the room and almost explode with laughter. We all look ridiculous. Each of us hinged forward in anticipation, a single index finger raised in front of our faces. Our eyes narrowed in concentration as if the world's existence depends on the words that will come out of Mason's mouth. Maybe there is a chance I could win this silly game after all.

"Never have I ever," Mason begins.

"Come on, Mason. We're not getting any younger," Grace teases.

"Had a stepparent."

I feel the spit stick in the back of my throat as an image of Frank surfaces. He is standing with his bulging belly, his beard unkempt, and eyes wild. *"Your mother's a whore, Billie."* I glance around the living room. I am the only one to put a finger down. The only child of a broken family. I have lost.

"Woot," Mason shouts. "I gotcha Billie!"

I don't like the way he says my name. He says it just like Frank always did, emphasizing the 'ie' with patronizing contempt.

"Shot. Shot. Shot," Grace and Mason cheer in unison.

Clare leans forward, pouring tequila into a shot glass. For the first time, I notice a tattoo on the inside of her forearm. I can just make out the words: *never forget who you really are.* Mason nudges the brimming shot glass towards me, his eyes gleaming. It is a challenge, I realize.

I snatch the glass from the coffee table, tilt my head back, and toss the liquid down my throat. The alcohol burns as it connects with the sensitive flesh. My eyes return to Mason's as I slam the shot glass back down.

Challenge accepted.

Grace and Clare cheer and clap. I smile but do not like the way the room is tilting. My stomach, filled with a mixture of beer, gin, and tequila, grumbles. The hunger, I managed to suppress earlier through sheer willpower, is returning in full force. I need to leave. This is dangerous.

My hands are braced against the love seat, ready to push myself to a stand, when Grace jumps to her feet. The alcohol seems to have imposed the opposite effect on her. She is filled with energy whereas I feel like a limp plant that someone forgot to water.

"Anyone up for a late-night meal? We could walk to Carl's Diner. Pancakes sound amazing," she says.

"I'm in," Mason adds. "What about you, Clare?" He nudges her elbow.

Her arms are now crossed in front of her chest, her tattoo hidden. "I'm pretty hungry too," she says. "I'm for it if Billie is?"

I turn to look at her. Sure, I'm starving. What they do not understand is what I am hungry for. My stomach grumbles at the thought of it. *Control yourself, Billie. You can fight this. You can be a typical twenty-nine-year-old man.*

"Please say you'll come," Clare says, a hint of pleading in her voice.

All it takes is one flash of those blue eyes. I cannot stand to disappoint her.

.   .   .

Carl's Diner is empty aside from a pair of truckers at an adjacent table. We are squeezed into a booth with splitting faux leather seats stained with smudges of dried maple syrup, and God knows what else. This time I beat Mason, sliding in next to Clare. Grace sits across from me, Mason beside her. My stomach erupts in obnoxious rumbles. I wonder if the others can hear it.

"I'll have the monster pancakes please," Grace chimes to the waitress who has appeared at our table.

"From the kid's menu?" The waitress asks, removing the pencil from behind her ear. She is an older woman, her face hardened with lines. Her bottle-blonde hair sits in a ponytail atop her head. If it was a different decade, she would have a cigarette dangling from her lips.

Grace nods eagerly, the buzz of tequila and beer swirling behind her brown eyes.

"I'll take the same," Clare blurts. Her gaze meets Grace's, and they burst into laughter understood only between them.

Both Mason and the waitress roll their eyes. "And for you two?" she asks.

"I'll take the bacon and cheese omelet with a side of home fries," Mason dictates.

"And I'll just have a coffee. Black," I add.

The waitress folds up her note pad and flees in a hurry. Working in an all-night diner, I imagine she is used to dealing with drunks like us. She has that no-nonsense attitude that is common among waitresses. Her only regret is probably not telling us to go fuck ourselves and sober up, but then she knows there'd be no chance for a tip.

"Billie, you're not getting any food. Aren't you starving?" Clare asks.

"I'm okay," I lie.

When the waitress returns balancing our plates in the crook of her arm, the smell makes me nauseous. She slides a steaming mug of coffee towards me and food in front of the others.

"This is too cute," Grace squeals.

I glance at the girl's plates and understand the relevance of monster pancakes. An enormous pancake is decorated with two banana slices for eyes and chocolate chips for pupils. A whip cream mouth is lined with fangs of strawberry slices and used again to represent horns. The sight is almost comical. Two grown women decked out in black, dark eyeliner, and piercings appreciating such a childish gimmick. I want to smile, but my hunger is too persistent. It sounds as if a thunderstorm is taking place inside my abdomen.

Mason steals a strawberry fang from Clare's pancake. I imagine myself leaping across the table, pinning him to the ground, and tearing his goddamn throat out as blood explodes onto my face in a hot stream.

Sweat forms on my palms. What would they say if they knew what lived inside me? Would they explode with shrill screams? Would they point their fingers in accusation condemning me a murderer? They could never understand that I need to take another's life to live. Not even Clare would be able to come to terms with what I have become. This is the tragic life of a monster. I am nothing like the silly pancakes that stare back at them with their lifeless chocolate pupils and strawberry fangs.

My stomach gurgles. I cannot think clearly. My head is still foggy with intoxication. *Hold it together, Billie. You can do this.* Normalcy is within arm's length. But my assurances are pointless—the Other has woken. The bottomless pit filled with jagged edges and sharp teeth will not lay dormant until it is fed.

"I've got to go," I announce. "I'm sorry. I'm… I'm… not feeling well."

Clare's hand juts out, latching onto my thigh. "Will you be okay getting home?"

I nod, but my mind is not concerned with getting home. My mind is consumed with the need to feed. I throw a half-hearted wave to the others. Billie wants to hug Clare and say goodbye or, at least, gently squeeze the hand that is still resting on my thigh. The Other, however, has another idea. The Other wants me to pull away from Clare, and if she tries to stop me, it wants me to tear her arm from its socket

I free myself from the booth and bolt for the exit. A rush of cool air slaps me in the face. I realize I forgot to pay for my coffee. The Other shuts me down, reminding me it does not matter. My feet feel unsteady. The world shaky.

Focus. Focus. Focus.

I need to find my way to the woods and disappear into the safety of the trees. I will be able to think out there. There will be no witnesses. My eyes dart around the quiet city and land on the face of a man. He walks by without a glance. I want to go left, away from Concord, but the Other commands me forward.

"Excuse me," I hear myself shouting, the words leaving my mouth without permission.

The man pauses then whirls around. "What's up, man?"

I can hear the slur in his voice. Just another guy enjoying a Saturday night in town. "You dropped your wallet."

"Really?" he asks.

The Other advances forward.

The man is patting his pockets, his eyes glazed with confusion. "No, it's right he—"

I seize him by the throat so tight he can't scream and force him into the alleyway behind Carl's Diner. A rat scurries away, and the smell of wet dumpster fills my nostrils. My fingers graze the edge of the box cutter in the back pocket of my jeans. I usually snap their necks. It is not fair they should suffer. But the Other does not share my morals tonight.

Do it. Do it. Do it, now, it commands.

The box cutter slashes out, slicing into the meat of the man's neck. He reaches for his throat in a poor effort to stop the bleeding. The Other is already there, lips curled around the wound, lapping up the warm liquid. The Other remains latched on even as the man collapses to his knees, then the pavement. It is not until the man's body gives a final twitch that the Other is satisfied and retreats.

Now, I am left alone, kneeling over the corpse of a stranger with blood around my lips.

CHAPTER 12

Fourteen Years Ago

Snowflakes swirled outside in a violent uprising. Wind rattled and shook the house. The wind chimes hung on the front porch sound in a frightening harmony. It was a bad one out there. The snow had already accumulated to seven inches, going on eight. It was a typical New England winter. Just another Nor'easter for the books. Clarice's grandmother, June, always said snowstorms are like sex. You don't know how long they are going to last or how many inches they'll be. It was not until recently, at fifteen, that Bill understood the joke.

"She's a fucking whore, Billie," Frank shouted while pacing the living room, a can of beer clenched in one hand as usual.

Bill narrowed his eyes but kept his mouth shut. When it came to Frank arguing, or even speaking for that matter, was pointless. Instead, Bill stared straight ahead at the muted television. His stepfather crossed in front of the screen periodically as he completed anxious laps around the couch. Hopefully, the storm wouldn't knock the power out. The last thing he needed was to be trapped with Frank with no television, no electricity, and no running water because the well pump shut off.

"Did you hear me? Frank asked, his pacing coming to a sudden halt. His eyes landed on the blue blast emitting from the television. "And what did I tell you about the T.V.? It'll rot your brain, and you don't have much of one to begin with." He hit the power button. The muted television fell dark.

Frank didn't let Bill have anything. He took his cellphone, threw his homework around the room, and threw the remote when Bill asked to watch a television show. Living in the same house as Frank was like cohabitating with a lion, never knowing when they could snap and go for your throat. Worst of all, Frank had sucked the life from his mother. Now she was just a shell of herself. The bags under her eyes had grown darker, and she stood up for herself less and less. It hurt Bill's heart to see her that way.

"She's up to no good. I just know it," Frank stammered.

Bill suppressed a groan. "No, she's not. She's just snowed in at the bar. She called an hour ago. You heard me talking to her. Ed said he'd take her home in the truck when it lets up a bit." Bill was worried too, but he trusted Ed to get her home. Plus, she had ended their conversation with *rose petals,* so he knew she'd be all right.

Frank scoffed. "Yeah, I'm sure she loves being snowed in with Ed, that fucking clown. I swear that woman will be the death of me. First, she ropes me into this marriage. Then, she leaves me with *her* snot nose kid, so she can go out and do God knows what with any Tom, Dick, Harry— or Ed."

Bill rolled his eyes. His mother was at the bar working another ten-hour shift contrary to what his stepfather imagined she was doing. Bill was positive his mother had never been unfaithful to Frank in the ten years they'd been married. Not that Bill cared. If anything, he'd encourage it. Maybe an affair would bring her to her senses, and she would finally leave the balding beer belly loser. Drinking seemed to make Frank paranoid. If his wife wasn't home, he could only obsess over the fact that he wasn't controlling her.

Frank crushed the beer can he had been holding and chucked it at the wall. The remnants of brown liquid tarnished the flowered wallpaper Bill had helped his mother put up the previous winter. A snap followed by a hiss of carbonation indicated Frank had already opened another can. "I'm telling you, boy... she's an untrustworthy whore," he said in between angry sips.

The word 'whore' filled Bill with rage. He was sick of hearing that same damn word every time Frank felt his ego deflate. "Just... just... shut up," Bill said.

Frank was behind him on the other side of the couch, but Bill felt the swoosh of air as he whipped around. "What did you just say to me?"

Bill's heart slammed against his ribs. He jumped to his feet, turning to face his stepfather. "I said, shut up!" This time he yelled it, screamed it at the top of his lungs.

Frank skirted the couch and stood directly in front of him. "You don't talk to me like that," he said while boring his beer glazed eyes into Billie's.

Bill had a growth spurt last summer putting him at almost six feet. Next year he would surely surpass his stepfather in height. He felt stronger too. Most of his peers would say he had the body of a nerd, but Bill disagreed. He had filled out in the past few months. Now, he noticed biceps when he looked at himself in the mirror. He held his ground.

"Did you hear me you little shit?" Frank asked, shoving Bill's chest.

Bill stumbled back but managed to regain his balance. Heat rushed to his face so fast, he could almost feel it turning red. His fists clenched by his sides. "Don't talk about my mother like that."

"Like what?"

"I don't want you calling her names anymore."

Frank chuckled. "Is that so? Well, what are you gonna do about it?"

Bill said nothing.

"That's what I thought. You're a pussy, Billie. You and your brother. It's not really your fault though. It's your mother's because she is a ball-grabbing, dick-sucking, worthless who—"

Bill cocked his arm back and swung. His fist connected with his stepfather's cheekbone, right below his glaring brown eye. The skin punctured. Blood spurted from the fresh wound.

Billie didn't have time to register the return swing. He wasn't even sure it happened until he heard the snap, the awful crunch of his nose breaking. His head rocked back as if his neck had been replaced with a slinky.

"You little bastard. I should kill you for that," Frank spat, bringing a hand to his wound. "Get out of my sight. I don't want to see your face for the rest of the night." Frank had told him to leave, but it was his stepfather who walked away. He retreated into the kitchen probably to nurse his injury with a cold beer can.

Billie collapsed onto the sofa, his head spinning with adrenaline. He should be crying. He should have pissed himself like a little baby. Yet his heart was pounding from raw excitement. Interlacing his fingers behind the base of his skull, he reclined as the blood from his nose pooled into his throat. It tasted of heavy metals, iron, and copper, but for Billie, it also tasted of victory.

Joy.

Elation.

For the first time in his life, he was living.

CHAPTER 13

My eyes flutter open, then shut. Sleep latches on threatening to pull me back into its embrace. There is a tingling sensation in my legs. My eyes pop open again. It takes a moment to realize where I am: my car, on the floor, curled between the passenger seat and dashboard. My head is cranked at a horrible angle against the glove box. Morning light filters through the car windows, and the distant chirp of birds bounces off my eardrums. Curse those cheerful little bastards.

I shield my eyes. My slamming headache is an unfortunate reminder of last night's alcohol consumption. A spasm shoots through my right leg and, for a second, I think I am unable to stand. The pain subsides, and I am left with only the dull sensation of pins and needles.

Hoisting myself onto the passenger seat, I peer through the window. I recognize the forest instantly. I am behind Gus and Darlene's house in my usual parking spot a few feet from the narrow stream. From the location of the sun, it is probably close to 7:00 a.m. How had I managed to make it home? I have only fragments of memories after leaving the diner. A flash of a man's face… the gleam of a blade… the taste of blood… rinsing my mouth in the park's fountain. After that, there is nothing. I have no recollection of the hour drive home. The fact I do not remember sends a shiver down my spine.

I heave the car door open. The expanding sunlight blasts me in the face and sends a lightning bolt of pain shooting into my brain. I need to lie down. I stagger my way from the cut out in the forest to Gus and Darlene's dirt driveway. The house appears quiet. I mutter a silent prayer that they are both still in bed. I continue forward, descending the hill to Every Penny Counts where my bed awaits.

        • • •

"Billie," a gruff voice calls, followed by three strong raps on my door. "You in there, kid?"

My eyes spring open, and I practically leap out of my cot. My heart slams against my ribs as if trying to escape its cage of bone and cartilage. For a moment, I am sure the voice belongs to Frank. He is pounding on my bedroom door, trying to gain entry to beat my ass for something he thinks my mother did. That is impossible though. I have not seen Frank in eleven years, and my mother is dead.

"Billie?" The voice is Gus's. "There is someone here to see you up at the house."

"What?" I call back. My heart, which just began to slow, resumes its unsteady rhythm.

"There's someone here to see you."

"Who?"

"A woman."

My head is still woozy. I stumble around my tiny room while pulling on fresh clothes and running a brush through my hair. I make a quick pit stop at the sink in the backroom to brush my teeth and splash cold water on my face.

A woman here to see me. Could it be a detective or someone from the local police department? The old man wasn't very specific, but surely, he would have mentioned if this woman was with law enforcement. I dash through the store, throwing a wave at the gangly high schooler Gus has working the register on my days off. The kid is a friend's son or else Gus never would have trusted him.

When I enter the kitchen, I find Clarice at the table sharing a mug of tea with Darlene and Gus. Compared to last night, her attire is more subdued. Her shoulder-length hair is in loose curls and tucked behind one ear, revealing a collection of piercings. A long-sleeved black shirt conceals the tattoo I had glimpsed on her left forearm. Her blue eyes sparkle against her darkly lined eyes as the corners of her mouth curl into a soft smile. "Hey, Billie," she says.

I respond silently, lifting my hand in a pathetic wave. Pleasantries have been momentarily forgotten. I cannot believe she is here, sitting at this table with my… my… what? Parents? Guardians? What are Gus and Darlene exactly?

My eyes find the digital clock on the stove: 2:00 p.m. I was asleep for seven hours. How long has she been here while I slept off my hangover carelessly in the store?

"Billie," Darlene gushes. "We are so happy to finally meet one of your friends."

"A nice one too," Gus interjects with a wink.

"It was such a pleasant surprise when she showed up this afternoon," Darlene says.

"How long have you been here?" I ask.

My question was directed at Clarice, but it is Darlene who answers. "Oh, I don't know. About an hour or so. We tried to wake you, but it seemed like you needed your sleep. So, we've just been chatting away. Clare was just telling us that you two were childhood friends. Neighbors."

My spit evaporates, my throat going cotton dry. What had she told them? Had she mentioned my family? My mother?

"Let me put on some more tea." Darlene pushes back from the table.

"No," I blurt.

Darlene hesitates. "Oh?"

"It's okay, I mean. Clare and I are going for a walk." I look to Clare, hoping to silently plead with her to accept my plan, but she is already nodding.

"Thank you for the tea, Darlene. It was nice to meet you both. Billie had only nice things to say about you two, and I have to say he's right."

"Will you consider staying for dinner?" Darlene asks. "That is if you're planning on spending the afternoon."

Both Clare and Darlene look to me. Their gazes penetrate my skin. I feel Clare's anxiousness for approval and Darlene's eagerness and excitement for new company.

"Sure," I reply, forcing a smile. "I don't see why not."

"Oh, wonderful!" Darlene exclaims.

Clare excuses herself and follows me outside onto the farmer's porch.

"What are you doing here?" I ask.

Clare fidgets with her fingers, chipping at the black polish on her nails. The sleeve of her shirt slides down revealing the end of her tattoo: *you really are.* "I had no other way of contacting you. You mentioned you worked here and, well, I wanted to make sure you were all right. You weren't feeling well last night. I thought you might've had too much to drink and then tried to drive home. My mind got the better of me, and I couldn't stop imagining you in a wreck on the side of the road."

I sigh, annoyed by my frustration and paranoia. "So, you drove two hours to check on me?"

She nods.

"Thank you."

"I only just found you, Billie. I don't want to lose you again."

A smile plays upon my lips. I reach out and take one of her fidgeting hands in mine. "I don't want to lose you either."

. . .

I lead Clare to my car tucked away in the forest. We drive ten minutes to a local swimming hole on the edge of the White Mountain National Forest. We dodge the running kids and family picnic baskets working our way to the back area of the rocky pond. The air is crisp, clearing up the residue of my hangover.

We dip our feet into the cool water. I threaten to push Clare in, and she runs away giggling. It is the perfect afternoon, almost like we are kids again, spending our summer vacation plotting the best way up the old oak tree in my backyard. It is funny how easy it can be to reconnect with someone, to pick up where we left off. We are older now. Things have changed, but the memories we share and our understanding of each other was never lost. Our afternoon together makes me wonder how we managed to lose touch. How I *ever* could have forgotten about her, leaving her behind in that old town after my mother died. It shouldn't have mattered that we drifted apart in high school. She was still my friend. Always has been.

We are back in the car. The sun is working its way into the western sky. Clare is mindlessly chatting while flipping through radio stations. I am enjoying the breeze sweeping through the open window. For the first time in a long while, I feel like myself, like Billie. I realize then Clare has stopped talking. I glance in her direction. Her eyes are lost in the dashboard as if she is reading something only she can see. That is not what she is doing though. She is listening. A news broadcast is airing. The harsh direct tone of the female reporter cuts through the car:

Residents of Concord are in a panic this afternoon after the body of twenty-five-year-old, Tucker Gleeson, was discovered early this morning. A dog walker spotted the body in the alleyway between Carl's Diner and Walgreens after his dog alerted him to the crime scene. Details have yet to be released. Police suspect Gleeson's death may be linked to the string of murders spanning from Barren to the North Conway area...

"Oh God, Billie. That's horrible. We were there last night at Carl's Diner. Can you believe it?" Clare says.

I do not respond. I am listening. My hands tighten around the steering wheel. *What have I done?*

As a precaution, residents are encouraged to limit time spent outside after dark. The one thing police known for sure, these attacks happen at night.

"Billie!" Clare screams.

A speed limit sign is in front of us. I jerk the wheel left, missing the bright white sign by inches. The Toyota's back end fishtails. I ease my foot on the brake and steer the car back into the safety of the yellow lines. I do not turn to meet Clare's gaze. I know I will see concern behind her blue eyes. I am concerned too. The news was so distracting, so horrible, I had forgotten I was behind the wheel.

"So—sorry," I stutter.

This week's weather forecast has replaced the news report. We are almost back at the house. My automatic headlights switch on. At the same time, the evergreens and birch trees bordering the road seem to expand. The forest I usually find comforting is suddenly constricting. I want to stop the car and run until I physically cannot run any further. If I do not, I fear the trees will extend into the road, engulfing me in their sharp branches and thorny needles before suffocating me. I ease the car around a bend, and Gus and Darlene's white farmhouse comes into view.

"I thought when there weren't any new reports about those murders that the killer had stopped. Maybe he moved on, or maybe he just gave it up," Clare says. "Why do you think this guy keeps killing? I just don't understand how someone can do that."

I pause, giving the question some thought. "I don't think it's as complicated as you think," I reply. "Maybe he just can't help himself."

CHAPTER 14

I hold the storm door open for Clare. The warm, inviting scent of home cooking greets us. A smile forms on my lips, lessening my anxieties. Walking into Darlene's house after she has been cooking never gets old or any less special. I do not need to eat. I just need to smell the food. It was something never present in my house growing up. My house smelled of cigarettes, old beer, and mothballs. The scent of home cooking was something I could only imagine other homes must smell like. A smell that must follow Martha Stewart into every room she steps into.

"There you two are," Darlene says. "Did you have a good time on your walk?" She is standing in front of the stove ladling warm broth over a steaming pot roast. The table is set with cream-colored plates flanked by polished cutlery and folded cloth napkins. There is even a bottle of decent looking red wine. Gus must have opened it, allowing it to breathe. Fresh cut lilies are nested in a vase at the table's center. Darlene has pulled out her arsenal. The whole presentation is beautiful, even though it is strange to see the table set for four instead of the usual three.

"We had a great time," I respond, attempting to push the lingering news story from my mind. *I almost killed us both by crashing into a speed limit sign. Oh, and did I mention I suspect the police may be on to me. Let me tell you, there are only so many people you can kill before you slip up and finally make a mistake.*

"Come make a plate while it's still hot. Gus, dinner!" Darlene shouts into the living room.

The darkened room is illuminated by periodic flashes of blue. A grunt from Gus confirms he must have fallen asleep in front of the television as he is prone to do.

Clare loads her plate with pot roast, green beans, and a heaping pile of garlic mashed potatoes. I take maybe a tablespoon each of potato and beans. Focusing on the pot roast, I cut myself slab after slab, hoping it will fill the pit I feel growing in my stomach again. This hunger is troublesome. It seems my time between feeds is shrinking. After what I just heard in the car—I am afraid it is too risky for me to hunt any time soon.

I pour each of us a sizable portion of red wine. I study mine a moment—blood in a glass. I gulp it down, the similarity conjuring fresh images of last night: Grace and Clare giggling over their pancakes, me bolting for the diner door, the confusion on the man's face as he grabbed at his punctured throat. I shake my head, reaching for the water pitcher instead of more wine.

"So, I'd love to hear more about how you two know each other. I know you mentioned you were childhood friends," Darlene says between bites of mashed potatoes.

"Billie and I were neighbors actually. We lived… what was it? Four houses apart?" Clare asks.

"Five," I respond after sipping my water. "You're forgetting about crazy Mrs. Kirken's house on the corner."

"That's right!" Clare exclaims. "Anyway, my family moved to Wolfeboro when I was six. Because we were the same age, and pretty much the only kids in the neighborhood, we became fast friends. I was hoping there'd be some other girls in the area, but I settled for Billie." Clare smiles. "We basically grew up together. It was nice to have someone else my age to play with. Bill's brother is six years older than us, so he always considered himself too much of a big shot to hang around."

"I didn't know you had a brother, Billie," Darlene remarks.

Sweat coats my palms causing the fork to slip from my hands. I anticipate her next questions. *Where is he now, Billie? How come you guys lost touch?* But she is too preoccupied with Clare's presence to ask anything further on the topic. Perhaps those questions will come later after Clare goes home.

Darlene brushes the corners of her mouth with a napkin. "Where are your parents now, Clare? Did they follow you to Concord?"

"No, they are still living in the old neighborhood in Wolfeboro."

"Do you visit often?" Gus chimes in.

"I try to visit once a month. My job can be demanding so I usually limit visits to weekends and, unfortunately when you're working a nine to five, Monday through Friday, those fill up fast. It's strange to go back. Not much has changed. Of course, my parents have updated a few things, but the neighborhood is very much the same. Even Billie's old house looks just as it did eleven years ago. The new people haven't done much in terms of remodeling."

Darlene directs her attention to me. "Where do your parents live? I'm embarrassed to say I have no memory of you ever telling me."

My heart sinks. I shove a whole slab of pot roast in my mouth to buy myself more time to answer. Did I dare tell them the truth? I have tried so hard to keep it from them, and one dinner with Clare is threatening to expose my secrets. Yet the more I think about it; the truth cannot be any worse than the *truth* they have decided. Hadn't Gus said something similar once? Imagined horrors are always worse than the real thing. They had essentially welcomed a stranger into their home. Who was I really trying to protect? Gus and Darlene or myself?

"My mother is dead," I say.

The weight of the statement affects everyone. Clare averts her eyes, casting them downwards towards her plate. Gus shifts back and forth in his chair. Darlene's mouth drops ever so slightly, but she makes a quick recovery saying, "I am so sorry, Billie. I didn't know."

I shove another slab of pot roast into my mouth.

"What about your father?" Darlene asks, her voice just above a whisper as if she is afraid of what the answer may be.

I shrug. "Don't know. He just disappeared. My mother remarried. Let's just say my stepfather and I never got along." My eyes dart to Clare. She is still staring at her food, stabbing at her mashed potatoes with her fork. I look away. "He's doing time at Berlin Federal Correctional Institution last time I checked."

Gus's eyes widen. "For what?" he asks.

I resent him for the question, yet I know he cannot help himself. When somebody goes to prison people cannot resist the what-is-he-in-for question.

"Manslaughter," I respond. The big M-word. Murder without premeditation, perhaps more commonly referred to as a crime of passion by the layman. Although there was nothing passionate about killing my mother and, furthermore, I am not entirely convinced it was not premeditated. Maybe Frank did not sit down and draw up a diagram, but he sure as hell could have guessed that beating the living shit out of someone day in and day out could result in injury. Maybe one day he'd get so angry, he'd reach for a kitchen knife instead of the belt.

I study Gus and Darlene, watching as the horrible realization dawns on them. It does not take a rocket scientist to connect the dots—my stepfather murdered my mother.

"I came home one day to find my mother dead." The images flood my head: my mother surrounded by a deep red pool, her body sprawled at an unnatural angle, the groceries she had brought home scattered by her feet. That is how I had known something wasn't right. I had seen the grapes. Some of them had rolled into the living room, forming a trail back to the scene of horror in the kitchen. "My stepfather came in a few minutes later. He screamed. I had never heard someone scream like that before." I shut my eyes as Frank's scream echoes through my head, rattling my brain.

"Oh, Billie," Darlene says.

My eyes pop back open.

"That's so horrible, honey. I can't even begin to imagine what that must have been like."

She is right. She cannot imagine, but I can. I still remember the smudge marks Frank's knees left in the congealing blood as he knelt over my mother, cradling her in his arms. I can still hear his crying and hushed nonsensical words as he cooed to her. I will never forget the look in his eyes as he turned to me, his strangled voice cutting through the room in terrifying accusation, "*You did this to her.*" But he was wrong. He did that to her. I had just returned from school. It couldn't have been me, but that would be just like Frank to not take responsibility. He was always blaming someone else.

"Frank, my stepfather, was convicted of manslaughter and sentenced to twelve years in federal prison."

"Twelve isn't enough for what he did," Gus grunts.

"No, it isn't," I agree.

"No time could ever be enough," Clare adds. She looks up from her dinner plate for the first time since the conversation started, her eyes glisten with tears.

"After that, I left Wolfeboro. I bounced around from town to town, odd job to odd job, until I met you guys."

"And we are so glad you did," Darlene begins. "You have been nothing but a light in our lives. You are practically a son to us." Her hand flutters to her lips.

I can tell she is worried that saying I am like their son will trigger me. Perhaps she thinks I will jump to my feet and scream that she could never replace my mother. Instead, I choke on my emotions. Hearing those words is exactly what I need.

I place the final slice of pot roast into my mouth before sliding away from the table. Clare's gaze finds mine. Her eyes are still wet and heavy with guilt. She must realize it is because of her that my life's tragedy has unfolded over mashed potatoes and green beans.

"Thank you for dinner," I say to Darlene. I place my dish in the sink and step outside onto the farmer's porch. Clare joins me a few minutes later.

"I'm sorry about that," she says.

I shrug. "It's not your fault. They would have found out eventually."

"It is my fault," she says, fresh tears materializing in her blue eyes. For a moment, it looks as if she will say more, but she bites her lip and chips at her nail polish.

I have a sudden urge to embrace her. I want to hold her close and run my hands up and down her back. Maybe our lips would even meet. I take a step back and shake my head.

"Billie," she begins. "I wasn't sure I wanted to ask you this because it might be too soon. I know we just reconnected and…"

I nod, urging her on.

"I got news that my grandmother passed. We knew it was coming, she hadn't been well. I know you loved her and… well… I was hoping you'd consider going to the funeral with me. It's Monday. Back home. I'd understand if you didn't—"

"I'll go," I interject. Maybe it is because I have finally told the story of my mother's death out loud, but I feel invigorated and relieved. Perhaps what I need now is a chance to return to my hometown and find closure. More importantly, how could I possibly let Clare down?

CHAPTER 15

Thirteen Years Ago

Bill's life changed for good after standing up to his stepfather during that snowstorm. Initially, Frank had tried to regain control of him. He had gone to Bill's mother raving that her boy was out of control, that he was a little asshole in danger of becoming a nothing someday just like her. But Bill had seen his mother smile, the tiniest upturn of her lips when Frank explained Bill had conked him one. From that day forward, he wasn't scared of getting into fights with his stepfather. His secret weapon—he liked the taste of blood.

One night when Bill couldn't sleep, he tiptoed down the hall to the bathroom. Using his hands as a cup, he drank endlessly from the faucet. It did little to help. Bill's eyes searched the countertop and landed on Frank's razor. He found himself reaching for it. His intention had only been to feel it in his hand, to focus on something besides the strange feeling growing inside him. He did not even realize he had run the sharp steel across his thumb until he felt the sting.

The razor clattered to the tile.

Bill studied the small wound, a series of thin red lines. He jammed his finger into his mouth. The faint taste of iron tickled his tongue. Elation saturated his heart, filling his chest with a comforting warmth. It was a sensation almost equivalent to the day he'd hit Frank. Something inside of him desired blood. Something that chanted for more, more, more.

Maybe that's why Bill continued to cut himself. Not often, just when he felt the need to take the edge off. In a way, blood and happiness had become entangled. He could not seem to experience one without the other.

Bill paralleled the back fence, following it past the old oak tree to the edge of the woods bordering his neighborhood. He sat in the warm grass drinking a soda. A meow roused him. Bill pivoted towards the direction of the call. A gray Tabby cat emerged from the trees.

"Hey there," Bill said.

The cat responded with another high-pitched meow. Bill pursed his lips, making those strange clicking sounds people think cats enjoy. The Tabby's ears perked. The feline meandered towards him, keeping at a safe distance.

"Come here, buddy," he said. When the Tabby was in reach, Bill scooped him up and cradled the feline in his lap. He ran his palm down the cat's back and gave it a scratch behind the ears. The tags around the cat's neck jingled. An up to date rabies vaccine and a name, Jasper, were engraved in thick letters.

"Hey, Jasper," Bill said. "Nice to meet you." The cat purred in response, brushing its whiskers against Bill's hand. As most interactions with cats often were, it was short-lived. When Jasper had his fill of attention, he wriggled free from Bill and sauntered into the woods. Bill smiled, wondering if he just made a friend

That night Bill was jarred from a restless sleep. It was happening again, that unsettling feeling in his stomach. The voice inside that demanded more, more, more seemed to have woken.

He stepped into the hall. From his doorway, he saw the bathroom was occupied. Yellow light leaked into the dark hallway from the crack beneath the closed door. It was only midnight. His mother would be at the bar for another two hours. It must be Frank.

Bill pressed his ear against the bathroom door. Sure enough, he heard snoring. Frank must be drunk, probably passed out on the tile floor or slumped across the toilet. Nice.

His hands flexed by his side. He *needed* to get in that bathroom, or did he? There was another option—he could go back to bed. He *should* go back to bed. What he wanted to do with the razor was wrong. Normal people did not go around slicing their fingers on purpose and sucking on the blood that came out.

He back-pedaling from the door, retreating to the kitchen. There, he pulled open the drawer where his mother stored the knives. A small steak knife was selected. Bill studied it. He shook his head. What was he doing? Why was he here holding this weapon?

Panic gripped him. Sweat broke out across his forehead. Suddenly, the room was too hot. Bill dropped the knife and backed away from the drawer. His whole body was on fire. His feet were slick with sweat causing him to slide across the linoleum. He recovered, unlatched the sliding door, and escaped into the cool night air. A cadence of crickets blared around him. He braced himself on his knees, his breathing ragged.

That's when he saw it. A gray blur of movement just off the side of the deck. Billie straightened as the creature stepped forward, his panic forgotten.

Jasper, the Tabby.

The cat purred, brushing its whiskers against his hand. Bill scooped him up. Jasper was fidgety, but Bill did not want to let him go. It was nice to have a companion. He always wanted a dog, but Frank would never allow, what he called, mangy mutts to live in his house.

Bill embraced the cat while focusing on slowing his pounding heart. *See, it's okay. Everything is okay.* Jasper squirmed in his arms. Bill brushed his hand over the feline's back, trying to soothe him. *That funny business with the knife in there was silly. He just lost his head for a minute. All he needs is some fresh air and—*

Jasper slashed Bill's cheek with his pointed claws. The sting was sharp. The rejection worse. Bill slammed the cat to the floor. Jasper did not move. A small line of blood trickled from the cat's mouth. Bill studied it a moment, then touched the red liquid to his tongue.

CHAPTER 16

Returning to Wolfeboro is like watching a movie, almost as if I am witnessing the trip through somebody else's eyes. The sensation began the moment I climbed into Clare's black Subaru and watched Darlene wave from her rocking chair on the farmer's porch.

The radio is loud, filling the silence between Clare and myself. We do not talk. We both know what is at stake by us returning. Our reputations. Our esteems. Our dignity. At just over 6,000 people, Wolfeboro is a small-town, and small-towns like to talk. It is not easy having your name attached to a murder anywhere, but especially in a place like this. Somehow, in places like this, the victim becomes the accused.

The hour-long strip of highway finally gives way, revealing more of New Hampshire's trademark desolate winding roads. Maybe the treacherous country roads are why the state chose their motto "Live Free or Die". I stare out the window watching a blur of colonials and ranches pass. I catch glimpses of Lake Winnipesaukee through gaps in the spruce and pine trees. I picture the people in their boats on the lake. They are probably swimming, tanning, sipping cold beers. They love a town that sends a surge of discomfort through my body with each moment I spend in it. As a child, I used to fear ever leaving this place, and now, I worry I won't be able to get out fast enough. Oh, the irony!

"Welcome to the Jewel of Lake Winnipesaukee," Clare says, as we zoom by another exposed patch of the lake.

I sense her uneasiness too. I see it as the corners of her mouth twitch into a forced smile, and her fingers tighten around the steering wheel. I reach out and pat her arm. It is the only comforting action I can think to do. I am supposed to be here for support, so I resist the urge to tell her to turn around like we both want to do.

"How does it feel to be back?" Clare asks.

"It feels… strange," I admit. "How are you feeling?"

She shakes her head. "I'm not worried about me, Billie. I'm worried about you. I've been back and forth countless times in the past eleven years. I already know how horrifyingly awkward it can be to see old faces. All of them staring at you with their goddamn hateful stares, gossip on the tips of their tongues. They can't wait for you to leave so they can talk about how different you look or how they doubt you amounted to anything just like they always thought you would." She snorts a laugh. "I needed you to come with me because you get me. It's selfish, I know. But I don't want you to be uncomfortable. That is the last thing I want."

"I'm fine," I reply. Although *fine* is far from the truth. My stomach flip flops as we take the familiar twists and turns towards our old neighborhood.

Clarice throws me a sideways glance. I can tell she isn't convinced. "What happened to your mom wasn't fair." Her eyes glaze over with a watery film. "I can't begin to imagine having to come back here and face that. I'm sure you wanted to stay as far away from this place as possible. I'm sorry if I made you come before you were ready."

"I am ready," I say. "I've been avoiding this town for eleven years. My brother is who knows where. Frank is in prison. Now, all that is left for me here is memories. And memories, well, they can't hurt me." Despite my anxiety, I believe it. Frank is my biggest problem, and if he is not here, there is no problem. Everything else is just in my head.

Clare smiles. A tear droplet trails down her cheek, landing on her upper lip. "I suppose you're right. I guess this is just my long rambling way of saying thank you."

We take a left onto our old street. Clare was right. The neighborhood has not changed. It is like a living time capsule, transporting me back to my youth. There is that same pothole on the corner. I hit it on my bike once and went flying over the handlebars onto the pavement tearing up my shins and palms. The street is flanked by the familiar neutral-colored houses no one has bothered to update in the past eleven years, except for crazy Mrs. Kirken's house. Her place is now a vibrant urine yellow.

I see *it* next. There is nothing particularly scary about the house. There is no looming hedge maze in the backyard. No sinister windows that could be mistaken for glowing eyes in the darkness like in *The Amityville Horror.* Yet the sight of it sends a shiver down my spine all the same. This house is not just any old box of wood mounted on cement. It was *my* house. The house I grew up in. The house my mother was murdered in. The house where the Other came into existence.

I cannot tear my gaze from the bungalow even as the memories flood back. I see my younger self climbing the front steps, the front door ajar. My mother's car is in the driveway. A cool breeze from the cracked windows greets me as I step inside. I notice the grapes scattered across the living room floor. There is confusion in my voice as I call her name, following the trail of grapes into the kitchen—

The car jerks to a stop. We are in front of Clare's, my house safely out of sight. I lift myself out of the Subaru and step onto unsteady legs. A pit sits heavy in my gut. It is not the usual pang of hunger I feel, but a ball made of dread.

"Are you ready, Billie?" Clare asks.

I nod, although I realize I might have been wrong about one thing.

Memories *can* hurt you.

PART II
FAMISHED

CHAPTER 17

CLARE

My worries concerning Billie are overshadowed by my anxiety as my parents emerge from their house. They must have heard my car pull up the gravel driveway. Damn that gravel, always giving me away.

They are descending the front steps, on route to meet us. I hoist my overnight bag over my shoulder and prepare myself. Running my fingers through my hair, I slip a brown strand behind my ear, knowing it will upset my mother to see it any other way. I do not bother to glance at Billie. I know he is as nervous as me. He has every right to be.

"Hi, sweetheart," my mother says.

She is all smiles. Her white teeth gleam between her painted ruby-red lips. She looks a little like a clipping from a *Home and Garden* magazine. A flowered dress hugs her slender frame which is supported by a pair of tasteful heels. Her dark brown hair, a shade identical to my own, hangs in soft curls. I almost wish she was wearing an apron and yellow dish gloves—that would really be a sight. I find the corners of my mouth rising into a grin because I do not expect anything less from her. Warmth pangs my heart. Despite what I told Billie and Darlene last night at dinner, I have not visited my parents in over six months. I did not even realize how much I missed my mother until my arms are around her.

My father is a different story. He hangs back, always the more reserved one. Most people would consider him a good-looking guy, but he dresses in sweaters that even Mr. Rogers wouldn't be caught dead in. He gives me a closed-lipped smile. It is the type of smile you might give the kid ringing out your groceries at the supermarket, not the smile you reserve for your daughter who you haven't seen in six months, maybe more. When my mother is through smoothing my hair and planting kisses on my cheeks, he steps forward. We embrace because we know it is what we are supposed to do. It is a quick hug. The secret we share passing silently between us.

Billie is a surprise. My mother's eyes widen when she catches sight of him by the car. "My goodness! Billie Dunne is that you?"

By the looks of him, I suspect Billie would rather hop back in the car and drive a million miles away than deal with Wolfeboro and the people in it. He steps forward and extends his hand to my mother. She bats it aside and envelopes him in a hug. I nearly breathe out a sigh of relief.

"What a pleasant surprise," she coos, now holding him at arm's length. "I can't believe how much you've grown. Look at you! You were just a boy when we last saw you."

Once again, my father hangs back. Only after my mother is finished hugging Billie does he extend his hand. "Billie, good to see you, kid," he says.

"It's great to see you guys too," Billie responds. His tone is lighter, or at least less intense than it had been on the drive.

"June would be so pleased you are here together," my mother says. "She always had a soft spot for you, my dear." Her finger juts out, connecting with Billie's chest.

At the mention of my grandmother's name, it hits me, the real reason I am back in this shitty town. This would be the first time my visit would not entail a trip to the assisted living facility my parents had moved June to a little over two years ago. Already her absence is felt. She had lived with my parents since I was born. It never even mattered that I did not have a baby brother or sister. I had my crazy grandmother to entertain me, and boy did she ever.

"Please come in. You two must be exhausted," my mother insists.

The drive from Barren to Wolfeboro was only an hour, but it is just like my mother to exaggerate. Imagining our drive to be more like a cross country trip will give her an excuse to nurture us. When she is busy doing that, there is no room for her to worry about her own life. Oh, how I envy her. If only my coping skills were half as useful. Why couldn't I be the type of person who cleaned the house when things got stressful? Instead, I tended to search for the answers to my problems at the bottom of a tequila bottle.

My mother apologizes for the house being messy. There are two issues with that statement. One, the house is not messy. Two, the house is *never* messy. My mother is a bit of a control freak. She cleans, she organizes, she throws your shit out because it's unneeded clutter. Her decorating is also a bit over the top. All the glass, chrome, and white carpets give the place a strange, modern feel despite being smack dab in the middle of rural New Hampshire.

With this kind of house, it is funny to think my parents had ever settled on a name like Clarice. Clare, as I go by now, would have been a better fit. Clare is a name for snobs. It has that perfect nasally sound to it. Girls named Clare eat vanilla ice cream, go to Saturday morning yoga classes, and have sex in missionary position. Clarice, on the other hand, conjures up a much different image. Clare is powerful. Clarice underconfident. Plus, no one can ever say it without thinking of Clarice Starling from *The Silence of the Lambs*. I am so sick of people quoting, "Well, Clarice, have the lambs stopped screaming?" No, goddammit, they haven't!

. . .

Dinner is a chore. We make tedious conversation with my parents. Billie hardly even touches his food. I notice my mother eyeing his plate. I can practically read her thoughts. *Is the food cold? Did I overcook the broccoli? Did he lose his appetite because my house is in such a state?* I try to distract her by asking about the garden, but my father's periodic grunts of input are unnerving. I find myself squeezing my fork so hard, my fingertips turn a ghostly white.

We help clear the table. Billie transfers plates from the dining room to the kitchen sink where my father scrubs and loads them into the dishwasher.

As I gather the water glasses, my mother brushes my shoulder. "Billie has turned into quite the handsome young man," she whispers.

"You think?"

"I do," she responds. "Maybe your grandmother was right. You were only children back then, but maybe you *would* be good together. Is he single?"

"It's not like that," I insist.

She chuckles. "Never say never."

I roll my eyes.

"You know," she begins, "when your father was young…"

At the mention of my father, my body tenses. Suddenly I am all too aware of the clinking dishes and the chatter between my father and Billie drifting from the kitchen. My throat goes dry. I know the only remedy is a drink.

"Mom, I'm really tired. Do you mind if I go change into pajamas?"

"Oh, of course not," she frets. "I put your bag upstairs in your old room."

I hurry up the stairs and down the hall until I am standing outside my childhood bedroom. My mother had cleared out most of the clutter. The dolls, stuffed animals, and books that had once been scattered throughout the room have been donated or packed away in neat bins in my closet. I study the four walls that I had painted a dark gray, covering the pale pink they'd once been in a moment of teenage rebellion. They seem so empty without the posters and sheets of handwritten poetry taped to them.

My overnight bag rests on a new duvet cover. Beneath it, I spot my old floral sheets, the same ones I had in high school.

I unzip my bag and dig beneath my folded clothes to reveal a small pint of tequila I'd stowed away. My mother does not believe in keeping liquor in the house. Don't get me wrong, she drinks, but she always maintained keeping booze on hand creates temptation. Maybe she is right.

I toss back a shot of tequila and divert to my closet, parting the accordion doors. My childhood is sorted, displayed, and labeled in clear plastic bins. *Barbies. Books. Baby Clothes*. My mother saved select things in case I want to give them to my own children someday or, at the very least, maybe sell a few vintage items on eBay.

A bin in the far corner catches my eye. *Poetry*. I peer inside and find some of the pieces I had written in high school. Skimming through a couple of lines, I smile. Memories of high school love, jealousy, and heartache preserved in notebooks written in looping cursive and colored ink. I dig deeper into the bin and spot my black journal. My heart does a violent flip flop.

The black journal is what I have come to think of as my book of darkness. It was reserved for my most intimate and unsettling secrets, translated into metaphors that no other person could decipher. My book of darkness was a home for the things that tormented me but could *never* say out loud.

Throwing back another swig of tequila, I drop to my knees, gripping the journal. I set the pint aside, take a deep breath, and open it. There is page after page of poetic verse. Some are full pages, others only a few words. Sporadic, random thoughts expressed with half-written sentences litter the white sheets in between. Towards the end, only single words are printed across full pages. Dirty. Liar. Scum. Undeserving.

Hot tears well in my eyes. A saline drop lands on the '*ing*' in undeserving. I wipe it away, smearing the ink. Turning the page, my eyes scan the sentences my younger self had written. *I watched the woman fall. She cried out and still I did nothing at all.* Those lines bring more tears, obscuring my vision with a watery haze.

"Clarice?" my mother says from behind.

I jump and slam the book shut. "Shit! You scared me," I say. I wipe my eyes with the back of my arm and turn to face her.

"I'm sorry, honey. What are you doing down there?" Her gaze falls to the pint by my knee, the corners of her mouth turn down.

I slide the tequila behind me. "Nothing really. Just looking through some of my old poetry."

"Anything good?"

I shrug. "Just silly high school stuff." The book of darkness burns in my hand. I place it back into the bin and rise.

"Well, I just wanted to let you know there are clean sheets on your bed. I left some blankets and pillows downstairs on the couch for Billie."

"What? Why does Billie have to sleep on the couch? Why can't he—"

"Sleep with you?" she finishes.

I nod.

"My house, my rules."

"But he's my friend."

"He is also a man."

"I already told you, it's not like that," I demand.

"Well," she says, "then it shouldn't matter that he's sleeping downstairs. He doesn't mind. I've already told him."

"I'm almost thirty-years-old."

"I wish you wouldn't have done that," she says.

For a moment, I think she is referring to me sneaking alcohol, then I realize she is staring at my tattoo. It is just like her to change the subject in an argument she can't win.

"You have such pretty skin. Why did you have to go and do that?"

I study my tattoo: *never forget who you really are*. I think back to the book of darkness. "Because I had to," I say. My throat constricts. I understand two things then. One, I need more tequila. Two, I can never let anyone else read that journal.

CHAPTER 18

Thirteen Years Ago

It was well past midnight as Billie patrolled the tree line in his back yard, listening for the crunch of leaves or the snap of twigs. After minutes of excruciating silence, he grew impatient. Turning from the woods, he ambled towards the road in need of a quick fix. A cat. A squirrel. Anything to cure the unsettling hunger building inside him. Sometimes it was so powerful, it was like another person or thing resided inside him.

Hitting the asphalt, Billie quickened his pace. He needed to hurry and finish this before his mother returned home from her shift at the bar. She could not find him like this. She already suspected there was something wrong with him. She thought there was some sort of gear stuck in his brain that prevented the machinery from running smoothly. Maybe she was right. It was why she'd been bringing him to all those psychiatrists, with the hope they could squirt some oil on those gears in his head and get them going again.

Bill did not like the doctors. They scared him with their psychology mumbo jumbo, their trick questions, and their fluorescent orange medication bottles. Some small part of him believed if he tried hard enough, he could get better on his own. He was sixteen, old enough to know that killing animals was wrong. But this *other* part of him justified that people kill thousands of animals every day just so they could enjoy a side of bacon at brunch. He, on the other hand, feared he would die if he did not get what his body craved.

"Billie?" A female voice called from behind.

Billie jumped. Who in the world was strolling down the road in the middle of the night? He whipped around, his heart slamming in his chest, to face Clarice.

"Is that you?" she asked breathlessly, jogging to catch up to him.

Bill nodded. After a few seconds of silence, he realized it was too dark for her to read his body language. "Yeah, it's me," he replied, raising his voice to be heard over the hum of tree frogs and crickets.

She had a pair of high heels clutched in one hand. Her long brown hair grazed the edge of her shirt that drooped to accent her cleavage. Even in the dark, Billie swore he could see the soft glow of her blue eyes.

"My friends dropped me off down the street so my parents wouldn't hear them pull up. They don't know I'm out." She chuckled. "There was this crazy party at Brett's. They'd never let me go to in a million years. I think I may be a little drunk. There was a ton of booze there." She paused, peering around the empty street. "If we get caught out here, we are totally fucked." She wobbled towards him with a big grin on her face. Grabbing him by the shoulders, she said, "Why weren't you at the party? Oh my gosh, Billie, you should've been there. It was so much fun!"

Billie was shocked by her touch, flabbergasted by her nonchalance. Since they started high school, she'd barely said two words to him, and here she was acting like they were still best friends.

"Yeah, it's a bummer I missed it," he said, although the truth was, he didn't get invited to parties like that. Parties like that were reserved for the cool kids, not the kids who were glanced over every day in the hallway like him.

"Hey, what are you doing out at this time of night anyway?" she asked.

"I'm looking for my… my… cat," Bill stuttered.

"I didn't know you guys had a cat. Did you just get one? Aw, is it a kitten?"

He nodded, this time taking advantage of the fact she could not decipher his body language in the dark.

"Do you want to hang out?" she asked. "For old time's sake? I know I won't be able to fall asleep just yet."

"Yeah, sure," Bill agreed, a surge of excitement shooting through his body at the proposal. "I suppose we can go to my house. My mom's at work for at least another two hours."

"No," she demanded. "Sorry. I mean, I just don't want to get caught. Maybe we can just hang by the oak tree in your yard. You know, the one we used to climb?"

"Are you sure? It's pretty cold out. I have the house to myself tonight. Frank is watching the game at my mom's bar which really means he is spying on her."

"Well, I guess if no one's home it's okay."

"I have popcorn."

At that, her hesitation transformed into the giddiness of a little girl. "All right. Let's do it! I've even got a souvenir," she said, reaching into her purse she revealed a small bottle of vodka.

.   .   .

Bill popped popcorn and filled tall glasses with soda. They switched on the television and watched *Signs* because it was playing on AMC. Snuggled beneath the blanket, they munched on popcorn and took turns sipping from the vodka, chasing it with generous amounts of soda, each of them trying to hide their grimaces.

"I've missed this," Clarice said. "High school is a crazy place. I think sometimes you forget about the people you care about the most. It's like the friends you should have, you ignore and the friends you shouldn't, become your life."

Bill shrugged. "I still consider you my friend. We just see each other less."

She kissed him then. Bill hesitated, expecting her to pull away laughing, claiming she was too drunk to know what she was doing. When she didn't, he leaned into her, surprised by how good it felt. How natural.

The kiss that he'd expected to last only a few seconds lingered into minutes. He envisioned lying her down, reaching under her shirt, and between her legs. He fantasized about entering her as she let out a soft moan. He stiffened as the wild thoughts consumed his mind

Light pooled through the window. Tires screeched in the driveway. Both Billie and Clarice jumped to a stand, the bowl of popcorn flipping onto the carpet. Two car doors slammed shut, followed by the sound of voices.

"Shit. My mom and Frank are home."

Clarice had gone rigid, her eyes wide like she'd seen a ghost.

"Don't freak. They won't care if you're here. My mom loves you, and Frank doesn't care if I live or die. We can just go to my room and finish the movie—"

"No," she said, eyeing the front door. "I've got to go. I'll let myself out the back." She wheeled around and bolted into the kitchen.

She already had the back slider open when Bill caught her wrist. "Are you okay?"

She did not respond.

"At least let me walk you home," Bill pleaded.

"I'll be fine."

"We just watched *Signs*. Aren't you scared aliens might try to get you?"

She turned to face him. "No, that is not what I'm afraid of, Billie."

CHAPTER 19

Clare

The clouds could not hold any more water. It started drizzling as I paced the bathroom drinking tequila. I let the water run so everyone would think I was showering. I ended up in the shower eventually. It was easier to remove my smudged makeup that way.

Now, the light rain has turned into an angry downpour, pattering on the roof like bullet spray from a machine gun. Periodic flashes of lightning illuminate the dark room followed by bellowing thunder.

I lie in bed, studying the plaster on the ceiling. When I was a kid, I could see shapes and pictures. Now, I just see lifeless swirls. Despite the tequila, sleep does not come easy. My mind is consumed with thoughts of murder, death, and all the horrible things I have somehow managed to repress. I try to focus on my grandmother. I pretend she is still alive and by my bedside whispering her stories to me. That woman did not tell the typical fairy tale either, not that I expected her to. Rather, June told cautionary tales of men who lost everything in the stock market, and woman who married for money, not love.

When I do manage to drift off, a loud rumble of thunder shakes the house waking me. I pull the duvet to my chin. I am a grown woman, and the sound of thunder still unnerves me. Huddled beneath the covers, I listen. The house is quiet aside from the soft hum of the AC. Soon the humming becomes movement, and the sounds of the old house settling imagined footsteps.

Another electric sizzle of lightning cuts through the sky. My childhood room illuminates only to be once again swallowed by darkness. A pop of thunder rattles the room. I whip off the covers and jump to a stand. "Thunder is just God bowling," I hear my mother say. *Well, tell him to keep it the fuck down then*, I want to scream.

I tiptoe down the stairs skipping the steps I know creak from years of sneaking out. Another flash of lightning reveals Billie's outline on the couch. I hover over him. "Billie, are you asleep?"

He lets out a muffled grunt followed by, "No."

I smile, knowing he is lying. Another crash of thunder causes me to jump. "I… I… can't sleep. Will you come up with me?"

"In your room?"

"Yeah."

There is a long pause before he rises. "Of course," he says, slinging a pillow over his shoulder.

He follows me upstairs through the darkness of my house. I slip into bed and hold up the blanket and duvet so he can climb in bedside me. The mattress dips from our combined weight. It is strange to have a man in this bed. Breaking my parents' rules makes me feel like a teenager again.

I face away from Billie, my back pressed against his chest, my butt against his groin. I sense him hesitate, his arm hovering in the air before falling back to his side. He has always been so awkward, so timid. I reach back and place his hand on my waist. Soon his whole arm is around me. I snuggle into him. Our bodies are so close it's almost as if we've become one. His breath is hot on the back of my neck. I have the sudden urge to roll around and face him, to climb on top of him and smother him in kisses like I did when we were sixteen. It is a surprising thought that is overpowered by tiredness and the lingering images of nightmares.

"I love you, Clarice." I hear him say just before my eyes shut, and I drift off to sleep.

CHAPTER 20

Billie

To say it is an appropriate day for a funeral would be an understatement. The air is cool for late summer. Clouds, that are still somehow plump with rain after last night's storm, stain the sky an ugly gray. A whistling wind whips through the trees sending loose leaves through the air. It is the type of day that sets the scene of every Edgar Allen Poe story. Miserable. Dark.

Family and friends dressed in black huddle around the open grave. They listen to a priest promise heaven and peace, things that are hard to envision on a gloomy day like this one. There are a few sniffles, a few tears. Most people remain composed. June was an old woman, her death expected.

From across the huddle, I spot my brother among the grievers. Seeing him causes my knees to weaken. I envision myself falling forward into the open grave, the ushers shoveling heavy dirt on top of me. "He's better off in there anyway," they'd say. "He can't hurt anyone down there."

I shuffle from foot to foot, fighting my instinct to turn and flee. Clare's warm hand finds mine. Her touch causes my feet to go still. My dedication to her is the only thing that keeps me rooted in place.

The ceremony comes to an end. Mourners take turns throwing clots of cold dirt onto the coffin. Some people choose to throw flowers which I find the nicer gesture. As I approach the grave, I am reminded of June and I's brief time together. Whenever I would go by Clare's house to usher her outside on a playdate, June would be in her chair on the porch, a glass of Scotch in one hand. "You're a good boy, Billie. You want some wisdom from old June?"

I would always nod, eager to hear what crazy advice she had to offer this time.

"Never kiss a girl outside when it's raining. You know why? This isn't Hollywood. Girls hate that shit. It will ruin their hair and believe me; they spend a lot of time on their hair."

I'd laugh. She'd wink.

"I hope you two end up together someday," she'd add. My ten year-old-self would wrinkle my nose thinking her an old fool. Flash to almost twenty years later, and I find myself praying that June was right. Maybe Clare and I really will end up together.

I toss in a single flower and wish her well. When I look up to where my brother had been standing—he is gone. I wonder if my mind had simply played a trick on me. Maybe he had never been there at all. That is the more probable explanation. It is just a combination of being back in this damn town and all this sadness that has caused me to imagine him.

I eye Clare among the sea of family and friends talking and making pleasantries. As I step forward, a man cuts me off.

"Billie?" he says.

I know then I hadn't imagined my brother. He is here, in the flesh, only a foot in front of me.

"It's been a long time," Fred says. The eyes belong to my brother, but the body is much older than I remember. Fred's belly has a slight bulge. The corners of his eyes are crinkled from years of smiling, although I cannot imagine how it is he did so much smiling after what happened to our mother and us.

I pivot in search of Clare, my pulse drumming in my neck. He shouldn't be here. Nothing good will come from it. Bad memories. The Other.

Fred grabs me by the shoulder, spinning me back around. "You're really just going to walk away from me like that?"

"What are you doing here?" I ask.

"I knew June too. The better question is, what are *you* doing here, Billie? Nobody has seen you in over ten years."

I shrug. "Clare asked me to come."

"Clare?"

"Clarice. We… we… reconnected recently."

"Well, that's sweet. Almost like an episode of *The Walton's.*"

"Almost," I reply.

"What about me, Bill? You didn't think to ever reconnect with me? You left eleven years ago and here you are, ready to leave me again."

"Everything okay here?" Clare appears at my side.

"Billie and I were just catching up," Fred says. "How are you, Clarice? I'm sorry about June."

"I'm okay given the circumstances. It's good to see you again, Fred."

Again? The word flashes in my head.

"We've got to get going," Clare says to me. "We need to head over to my cousins for the reception. Will you be joining us? Her place is right in town," she asks my brother.

Fred shakes his head. "No, I can't. I was hoping to have a quick moment with my brother before you go though."

"Of course," she says. "I'll be in the car."

When she walks away, Fred asks, "Can we grab dinner sometime? Maybe catch up."

"I don't know, Fred."

He sighs. "Me and you were always a team. I guess I was just hoping, I don't know…"

I think of all the times Fred had my back or at least tried to have my back. The big hugs he gave me when he'd come home to visit after moving out. The moments he had stood up to Frank, taking one in the face instead of me. Fear is getting in the way again. Reconnecting with Clarice was such a positive experience maybe it would be the same for my brother too. "All right," I agree.

Fred breaks into a big boyish grin. We make plans to meet next week at a restaurant in Concord. We say our goodbyes, pausing awkwardly, unsure if a hug is appropriate.

I watch Fred walk away; my eyes unable to leave my big brother as he zigs-zags through the tombstones. I follow his form until it disappears outside the cemetery walls. Clare beeps the horn rousing me from my trance.

Funeral party. People do not like to use the word 'party' in conjunction with funerals even though it has all the elements of one. There is food, drinks, laughing, and crying. Some folks even wind up a little too buzzed for the occasion.

Friends and family are scattered throughout the kitchen and living room. Some linger outside smoking cigarettes and talking despite the cool breeze and air that smells of more rain. Most people are in good spirits, a few shed tears and expel a combination of sadness and snots into tissues.

I find myself in the living room with a Dixie cup portion of wine clutched in my hand. I am surrounded by people I do not know, yet some of them seem to *know* me. They throw curious glances in my direction, only bothering to avert their gaze when our eyes lock. Their voices fall to whispers as they murmur among their group. I can only imagine what they are saying. In a matter of minutes, my meager portion of wine disappears.

I search for Clare, but she is nowhere to be seen. As I contemplate whether to replenish my drink, I feel a gentle tug on my pant leg. A small toddler with curly auburn hair stares up at me. When I meet her bright blue gaze, she breaks into a giggling smile.

"Well, hi there," I say.

The child fixates on me with unwavering curiosity. Ice shoots up my spine with such intensity it is like I have been stabbed with a hypodermic needle filled with a paralyzing agent. Perhaps the toddler's innocence somehow allows her to see me for who I really am. Perhaps she can sense the Other begging and pleading to be let out. I shake my head, clearing it of the foolish thought.

I bend down. "What are you doing down there?" I ask the child, who still has a hunk of pant leg bunched between her chubby fingers. Suddenly, the tot is hoisted into the air, her grip on my trousers releasing.

"Sorry about that," the woman holding the toddler says. "That's the terrible twos for you. They get into everything. Touch everything. Eat everything. I can't take my eyes off her for a minute."

"It's no problem," I reply.

The woman has bright blue eyes that match the child's. They also remind me of Clare's. She must be her cousin.

The woman chuckles. "Some people call it the terrible twos, others the terrible threes. To be honest, I'm not convinced the terrible phase is over until they are at least eighteen." She nods to an older child seated on the couch. The girl, who looks to be about seven, has her face glued to an iPad armored in a pink case.

"You must be Clare's cousin," I say.

She wrinkles her nose. "Clare?"

"Clarice." It seems my friend has two separate lives. Those who call her Clare are part of her "new" life while those who still refer to her as Clarice are phantoms of her past.

"Yup, I'm the cousin," she responds. "Erin. You are?"

"Billie," I say. I notice the quick widening of her eyes.

"Billie, that's right. You're Clarice's friend. You guys were neighbors?"

"That's right."

She studies me a moment, surely recounting the horror story attached to my name. "This… this… is Mia," she says, taking the child's chunky wrist and miming a wave.

I return the gesture.

"Well, if you'll excuse me. I need to go mingle. It's nice to finally meet you, Billie."

"Likewise," I respond, but Erin has already dispersed into the crowd.

I make my way to the bathroom only to find it occupied. After a few minutes of waiting, a woman brushes by and suggests I use the one upstairs. I spot the bathroom at the far end of the hall. I relieve my bladder and funnel back the way I came. I pause in front of what I guess is the toddler's bedroom. It is painted a pale lilac and butterfly themed. I smile, remarking how bright and cheerful it seems in comparison to all the black and tears downstairs.

Returning to the living room, I refill my wine cup and sit on the far end of the couch, away from Erin's other child who is still lost in the world of electronics. People have gathered in a small huddle before me. I listen as they share stories of June and tip their paper cups in her memory.

"June was always such a hoot. That old bat was filled to the brim with wisdom," a woman, who by her age, was probably a friend of June's says.

"Wisdom?" a man interjects. "I suppose that would be the polite thing to call it."

The group laughs in unison.

"Remember how she'd always tell that story about her and her father?" the older woman asks.

A few people nod their heads.

"Well, June's daddy always bugged her when she'd leave the house with her coat unbuttoned in the winter. He'd say, 'Junie, button up that coat of yours, or you'll catch your death.' And June would respond, 'Daddy, if I button my coat how will the boys see my breasts?'"

The group falls into hysterics. I find myself smiling too. That was June for you, a spitfire even as a teenager.

.   .   .

The reception lasts well into the evening. Clare's mother busies herself with domestic tasks like packing leftover food into containers, clearing plates, and wiping down counters. I watch Clare roll her eyes and take sips of tequila from a small bottle in her purse when she thinks no one is looking. I raise my eyebrows at her from across the room. She smiles.

"Busted," I say to her as I approach.

"Give me a break, they were handing out Dixie cup sized glasses of wine," she replies.

"You noticed too. Perhaps they were encouraging moderation." I grin.

"Or they just wanted to save money. Either way, my grandmother would be so disappointed," she says. "You know what? Let's go get some real drinks in her honor."

I agree. We move through the thinning crowd, say our thank you's to her cousin, and disappear into the night.

CHAPTER 21

Clare

I suspected going into town would entail running into one or two old acquaintances. I hardly expected a high school reunion, which is almost exactly what it was like stepping into The Woodline Pub. The only things missing: a bowl of punch and half-assed decorations. Well, I suppose the decorations are half-assed. Although I envisioned more glitter and streamers as opposed to rustic farm equipment and moose heads mounted to the walls.

A group of girls I half know are sitting around a table in the corner gabbing. A few guys, who were once high school football stars, idle by the bar throwing darts. I notice a few other familiar faces scattered among the crowd.

I B-line for the bar with Billie in tow. My eyes never leave the line of tequila bottles lined up behind the bartender's head. The taste of salt and agave is in my mouth before I have even uttered my drink order, tequila on ice with lime. It is only after I've ordered that I realize I know the bartender too. Molly Dickenson, an old high school acquaintance. She recognizes us. I can tell by the way she hinges forward and rests her forearms on the bar top. It is body language that screams: *Hey, I know you, and I'm ready to talk your fucking ear off.*

"Hey, Molly," I say. "I didn't know you worked here." Obviously. I haven't been to The Woodline Pub in years.

"Clarice. I thought that was you. You look so… different."

I feel her gaze run over me like a thousand tiny needle pricks across my skin. She begins at my torso, her eyes pausing on my tattoo, before landing on my face where she studies my nose piercing and dark plum lipstick bordering on black.

Molly leans even further across the bar. "That Billie Dunne?" She asks it loud enough that I know Billie can hear, but she isn't asking him, she is asking me.

"Yeah, it is. Bring him a whiskey," I reply.

I realize then I've made a mistake. That night at The Den, Billie had been drinking gin. Stupid for me to think I should still know what he likes. As my mother said, Billie was just a kid when we last saw him.

In between her shuffling and snarky remarks to other patrons, Molly finally returns with our cocktails. I sip from my glass eagerly.

"So, what brings you guys back to town?" Molly asks.

"My grandmother passed. Billie's here for support."

"You guys kept in touch all these years? Weren't you neighbors growing up?"

"Yes," I say. No need for further clarification. For all she knows, the 'yes' is to both. I do not like her demanding tone any more than I like the way she directs her questions only at me as if Billie doesn't exist.

"Well, isn't that sweet. Are you two like *together* now?"

I pause, wanting her anticipation to grow. I can already hear the tidbits of gossip forming on her tongue. *They kept in touch all these years… she is totally fucking him… you should have seen how she looked dressed in all black with a tattoo.*

Finally, I shrug. "Just friends. Always have been." I give Billie's hand a quick squeeze beneath the bar.

"Right," she says, her eyes narrowing. "It's a shame you haven't been back sooner, Clarice. You could have livened up this crowd a bit." She peers around the pub. "I mean you and me, we used to be pretty close. A lot of good times shared between us. Do you remember that party at Matt's house? Oh my God! You were so shitfaced. You did a shot of vodka then backflipped into his pool on a dare. Gosh, the boys went wild for that."

I nod, vaguely remembering the party. I had gone with a couple of my girlfriends. It was the last big shindig of the summer. Brett Cushing was there along with most of the football team. I had been trying to impress him, and it worked. By the end of the night, we were making out in one of the upstairs bedrooms. I had even let his roaming hands wander under my shirt and between my legs. What had I been thinking? Backflipping into a pool when I was probably two times over the legal limit to impress a boy. My tiny sixteen-year-old body filled with cheap beer and raspberry flavored vodka. The one thing I do not recall about that night—Molly Dickenson. In fact, the only thing I can remember about her is the guys chanting in the hallway, "Molly, do you want my Dick…enson?"

"I agree. Good times," I say. I down my drink and order another for myself and Billie. When Molly returns, I snatch the glasses and lead Billie to a booth. I ignore her desperate stare knowing it is the only way I can dodge more teenage memories.

"That was horrible," I say. "I'll never understand why some people never move on from high school like it was the highlight of their life." I glance back at Molly. "Well, for her maybe it was."

Billie is unfocused. His eyes dart around the pub, holding his glass in a vice-like grip. I rest my hand on his forearm. "We can leave whenever you want," I say. "I just needed a few drinks. My mother doesn't believe in keeping booze in the house. A decision my grandmother frowned upon as you can imagine."

"I wish my mom had enforced that," he says.

I look down not wanting to meet his gaze, afraid my comment may have opened a bottle that may be difficult to close.

When I glance back up, he is smiling. "That was Molly Dickenson, right?" he asks.

I nod.

"What did the guys used to chant to her in school? Molly do you want my Dick…enson?"

"You're forgetting the extended version."

"Which is?"

"Molly's dad is a big old prick because of it there is nothing she won't lick. Molly, do you want my Dick…enson?"

We both burst into laughter.

"Clarice?"

I turn to find Brett Cushing standing in front of our booth. I hadn't noticed him when we arrived. Perhaps he had been concealed by the pack of empty-headed jocks shooting darts.

"I didn't know you were in town," he says.

The heat of what must be a blush stains my cheeks. I realize my hand is still on Billie's and I pull it away. I don't know why I do it. Brett Cushing is my ex-boyfriend and a high school one at that. "I'm here for my grandmother's funeral," I say.

"I'm sorry to hear that," he replies.

I smile despite myself. Brett has been the first person to offer any kind of condolences. Molly had just skipped over the topic entirely, more interested in pumping me for the scoop than my dead grandma. "Thanks," I reply.

"Hey," he says, regarding Billie. "How's it going, man?"

"Not bad," Billie responds. "And yourself?"

"I can't complain. I took over my dad's logging company awhile back. It's doing really well. Just bought a house by the lake. My next goal is a boat."

"Are you married?" I ask. A question that surprises even me.

"No, not yet. I guess I haven't found the right girl," he responds with a wink.

I feel a spark of satisfaction. The old pang of jealousy diffuses, not that he owes me anything. We broke up right after graduation. I told him I had been accepted into the University of New Hampshire and was moving on campus. It was only an hour away, but Brett couldn't handle it. He broke my heart. Looking back, it was probably for the best. He would have been a lousy husband. I remind myself of this as I study him. He looks almost exactly as he did ten years ago. The same dark eyes and hair. The same athletic build and chiseled superhero jaw. It is the similarities that make it easy to overlook what is different. The beginnings of a beer belly. A heavy five o'clock shadow. The tiniest bit of gray flecks scattered throughout his hair.

"What have you been up to, Clarice?" Brett asks and slides into the booth next to me.

Heat flames my cheeks again. I am suddenly overwhelmed by the situation. No one would ever want to be shoved into a box with a bunch of people from high school who they haven't seen in over ten years. Yet, that is exactly what is happening. I reach for my tequila and toss the liquid down my throat.

I briefly tell Brett about school and my new job careful to skip over my failed romances. When he asks about my parents, I reach for my drink instinctively.

Brett eyes my empty glass. "Hey, Billie. Would you mind getting us another round? On me, of course." He reaches into his wallet and reveals a crisp twenty-dollar bill. "Get yourself something too."

Billie studies the bill. For a moment, I am sure he is going to slap it from Brett's hand. "Sure," he says finally, taking the twenty.

Billie is always too polite. I try flashing him a casual sorry-this-guy-is-a-dick-smile, but he is already heading for the bar. I see Molly poke her curly head up, intrigued that Billie is making a solo booze run. She eyes Brett and me in the booth. Her lips twist into a smirk. *And then she ditched poor Billie for Brett Cushing. God, she is such a slut*, I imagine her saying.

Brett's hand grazes my thigh. I inch away from him. It is obvious now. From the moment he approached, Brett has been scheming up a way to get us alone. "Listen, Brett, it's been nice to—"

"Well, if it isn't little Billie Dunne," someone announces near the bar.

I see Matt Meyers stumble forward from the pack of ex-jocks. He is an old friend of Brett's or, perhaps more appropriately, a minion.

"I'm surprised you have the nerve to show your face around here after what you did," Matt slurs, his voice rising above the low hum of classic rock. The pub hushes. The blur of drunken chatter dilutes to excited whispers. "How's it feel to know your shitty stepdaddy got put away for your crime?"

"Fuck off," Billie responds.

"I *need* to get over there, Brett. Excuse me," I say.

Brett glances towards the bar. "You worried about him? He's fine. Matt's just rousing him a little, that's all."

"Like I said before, it's been nice catching up, but I have to go," I insist. I lean forward trying to get a better view of Billie. He is still at the bar now angled towards Matt and his gang of approaching idiots. He looks so small compared to them. I watch as a Jolly Green Giant from the back, his name might be Tom, steps forward. Then, my view is blocked by Brett's shoulder as he places his forearm on the table, pinning me in the booth.

"I told you not to worry," he says.

My jaw tightens. I cannot believe I used to like this guy, that I lost my virginity to him in his stupid blue Cadillac. "Brett, move," I respond.

"Dude you were such a loser in high school, Jeffrey Dahmer wouldn't even have wanted to be your friend." I hear a booming voice, which must belong to the big guy, say.

"Please, move," I ask again.

"Hey Billie, you've heard of a MILF, right?" This time the voice is Matt's. "What about a MILM? Mother I like to murder."

A few onlookers gasp. Someone in the bar shouts, "That's enough, boys". Then, there is the sound of a bottle breaking, accompanied by the patter of glass shards littering the floor. There is a loud crunch as someone takes a step forward.

"Fucking move," I yell as my fingers close around Brett's beer glass.

Brett laughs. I toss the liquid in his face. When he reaches for his stinging eyes, I wiggle out of the booth and hoist myself over the table. My feet hit the sticky wooden floor, and I am running towards Billie. A darkness has settled on his face. His eyes are narrow slits, his mouth a thin line. My hand finds its way into his clenched fist. I pull him towards the door, away from Matt, the maniac clutching a broken beer bottle. They call after us, saying things with no purpose other than to hurt.

"Freak."

"Weirdo."

"When you go to hell, tell your mommy we say hi."

The door swings open and cold air blasts us in the face. The sound of applause leaks through the pub's walls. I frown knowing Brett is among the clappers. I lead Billie to the car, and he collapses into my arms. I shake him off. "We need to get out of here, Billie." *Before they come outside and kick your ass*, I want to add but hold my tongue. I fumble with the keys in my pocket. I realize my heart is pounding, my pulse drumming in my neck. As I reach for the car door, Billie catches my trembling hand.

"What if they're right Clarice?" he asks.

"Those boys haven't been right about a thing in their lives."

"No," he says with frightening desperation. "What if they're right about my mother? What if I did kill her?"

I turn to face him. "That's impossible, Billie. You were at school. Your mother... she'd been dead for at least an hour before you found her."

"You don't know that."

"The police said so themselves."

"But what if they're wrong?"

"They are *not* wrong. You didn't do it," I say in my sternest voice although tears sting the corners of my eyes. "Now, we need to get out of here." I pull open the car door and slide in. Billie moves around to the passenger's side but stops. I turn the key, and the engine hums to life. Fleetwood Mac's *The Chain* softly fills the Subaru.

Billie is still standing outside, staring at the bar. Rolling down my window, I eye the front door half expecting to see Matt and an angry mob stumbling into the parking lot with torches and pitchforks. "Billie, for God's sake, get in the car."

He peers into the car. "I think I'll walk."

I sigh. "Please, just get in the car."

"I'll be fine. I just need to think."

I want to protest, but I can tell his mind is decided.

"You don't know everything about me, Clare. I'm not the person you think I am. I've done bad things," he says.

I watch him exit the parking lot and disappear down the dark street. "I've done some really bad things too," I say as I throw the car into reverse.

CHAPTER 22

Billie

Sticks and stones can break my bones, but words can never hurt me. Ha! What a laugh. Words will *always* hurt you. That is what the saying should be. A punch in the face is quick. Sure, it hurts, but you get over it. Words, on the other hand, they cut like knives. Sharp, tiny slashes that are sore and stinging, leaving you with scars long after they are said. And if you cut too deep, well, it might just kill you.

Mother I like to murder.

I replay Matt's words in a mechanical loop as if they have been dictated into a recorder that I am holding to my ear, hitting the play button over and over.

The belief I killed my mother is an unpopular one. Everyone with a brain cell knew the violence Frank was capable of long before he lost control and cut my mother's throat. The fact that people would even consider I had anything to do with her death sickens me.

Maybe that is why I turned back, retracing my steps down the dark, quiet street and reemerging in front of The Woodline Pub. There, I walked to the edge of the parking lot and entered the woods where I now sit concealed within the overgrown grass and saplings. I have a direct line of sight to the front entrance. I listen to the distant sounds of laughing and music as I continue to replay Matt's disgusting statement in my head.

.   .   .

One thing I remember from high school, most of the jocks were secret cigarette and pot smokers. It's ironic really. You would think it would be the opposite. Nerdy kids with socially empty lives like myself, their bodies primed for nothing more than to hunch in front of computer screens and math homework, that would indulge in smoking. Something simple to pass the time. Yet, strangely, it always seems to be the active kids who are the ones sneaking beers and smokes. Matt included. He used to sell Marlboros to the underaged kids in the parking lot after school. I am counting on Matt's continued nicotine addiction now as I sit and wait.

Minutes tick by in excruciating intervals. I watch as a few glassy-eyed patrons stumble into the parking lot. They fumble with their keys, laugh, and discuss who is sober enough to drive home. Some of them just choose to walk.

My heart palpitates as Matt Meyers emerges from the pub next, sure enough, a pack of cancer sticks clutched in one hand.

"Your next beer is on me, asshole," someone screams after him. Then, the door swings shut, muting the chaos of the pub. I study the entrance, waiting for one of Matt's goonies to follow, but no one comes. Just like high school, Matt is left alone. He may have been one of the popular kids, but he was always living in Brett Cushing's shadow. He was someone who floated on the edge of the popularity circle. Easily disposable. He was there just so the ring leaders had someone to boss around, and Matt eagerly awaited their commands hoping the next opportunity would win him some respect. Maybe that was what tonight's stunt with me had been. Another chance to impress his friends.

Matt strolls to the side of the pub where a stainless-steel ashtray stands. I feel the Other clawing its way up, climbing from the dark depths of my stomach into my throat. It is the first time it has made an appearance in a personal matter. Usually, it just shows up when it is hungry. My knees bend, ready to sprint towards Matt and pin him to the ground. *Focus,* I remind the Other and myself. Violence is not my goal.

I emerge from the woods, zig-zagging through the parked cars until I am standing a few feet from Matt. The parking lot light shines on half his face, the glow from the cigarette ember illuminates the other half as he inhales.

"Billie?" He squints, exhaling a puff of smoke. "What the hell are you doing here? I thought you left with your girlfriend."

I do not respond. His words are still on repeat. *Mother I like to murder. Mother I like to murder. Mother I like to murder.* My fists clench by my sides.

"What do you want, asshole? A cigarette?" He extends the pack of Marlboros, a gesture that surprises me.

"No," I say. "I want you to apologize." If he says he is sorry, even if he doesn't mean it, I will leave. I just *need* to hear him say it with the hope it will erase the horrible words stuck on repeat in my brain.

He ignores me. Taking another drag of his cigarette, his drunken eyes search behind me. "Is Clarice with you?"

Again, I do not respond.

"Did she go home with Brett?" He pauses. "I guess I'll take your silence as a yes." He chuckles. "Dude, I bet Brett is giving it to her so good right now. She probably has those sweet lips of hers wrapped around his—"

"Apologize!" I yell.

Matt flinches. "Jeez. You're serious? You want me to apologize for what happened back inside?" He hooks a thumb towards the pub.

I nod.

"All right," he says. "What we said about Jeffrey Dahmer not wanting to be your friend wasn't cool, but probably true." He smirks.

"You know that's not what I mean," I shout.

"Whoa," he says. "Listen, in all seriousness, I shouldn't have said that stuff about your mom."

I feel myself relax, my fingers uncurling from their fists, my heart slowing to a normal rhythm.

"It wasn't fair for me to say you murdered her." He takes a step forward, our bodies no more than a foot apart. "What I should have said is that you slit her fucking throat and danced in her blood, you psycho. For all I know, you probably raped her cold, dead corpse."

For a moment, I do nothing. I cannot move. I am shocked by his lack of empathy. How is it the worst day of my life, the day my mother was killed, has turned into a freak show for the residents of Wolfeboro? It has become nothing more than innuendos, secrets, and sneers.

Matt smiles. My muscles release from their atrophy. I reach out and slap the cigarette from his dumb smirking mouth.

"You little shit," he shouts, pushing me hard.

I fall backward, my elbows connecting with the pavement. Before he can throw a punch, I bounce up and flee to the back of the building. I am faster than him just like in high school. I picture all the times Matt pushed me against lockers. The way he would turn back and mutter, "Loser." It was nothing serious, nothing too violent, but just enough to let me know he hated me. I was an easy target to take his frustrations out on.

My fingers find the handle of the box cutter in my back pocket. I listen to the huff of breath as he approaches, the unsteady patter of his footfalls. He turns the corner, a shadowy figure in the darkness. The box cutter jerks out and slashes. A horrid gurgle follows. Matt's shadow hand reaches frantically for the wound. The cigarette he had retrieved, drops to the ground, the tip glowing by his sneaker. Matt's outline falls to his knees, then backward onto the pavement.

"I just wanted an apology," I say to him. *But, I admit, you are full of good ideas. Maybe I'll dance in your blood, I think.* I glance around the parking lot, not a soul in sight. I grab Matt by his shins and drag him to the edge of the tree line. The soft gurgles tell me he is still alive. I lean forward and look into his eyes. I want to see if he is sorry for what he said now.

He is attempting to speak. I inch closer, my ear hovering above his bloody mouth.

"You… fucking… killed… her…" he whispers before taking his final breath.

I study his corpse. The sight of his blood disgusts me. It is a poisonous black that is filled with hate. The Other does not share my feelings. It will never pass up an easy meal, especially when it has been so hungry. My jaw begins to click.

No! No! No!

I want to sprint away, but it is too late. The Other lunges forward and tears into Matt's throat.

·　　·　　·

I retrace my steps towards the far end of the parking lot, stopping only to stamp out Matt's cigarette now that the human part of me as been regained. Why let a small ember become a big flame?

Fifteen minutes into my walk, I pause to discard my blood-stained suit coat in the woods. I dig a small hole, deposit my coat, and cover it with dead leaves. A shallow grave for my funeral attire. How ironic.

I return to Clare's. She meets me at the door and wraps her arms around me. I pray the smell of cigarette smoke is masked by the scent of fresh air. As she releases me from her embrace, I spot a single drop of crimson blood on the tip of my dress shoe. A thin sweat breaks out on my forehead. Clare does not see the blood. Nor does she notice my missing suit coat, or the dirt beneath my fingernails. Sometimes I think people only see the details they want to see. Sometimes it seems people would rather ignore the facts than face the truth.

PART III
RAVENOUS

CHAPTER 23

Billie

A week after Clarice dropped me off in front of Gus and Darlene's white farmhouse, I am back in Concord to do something I thought I would never do again: have dinner with my brother.

I cross the street cutting through the same park I had been sitting in when I had spotted Clare and her blonde friend, Grace. That day seems so long ago, so distant. The week has trudged and dragged its feet like a child being towed to the doctor's office for shots.

My silent battle with the Other continues. So far, I am winning. I have not fed or hunted this week. After killing Matt, I am more ashamed than ever of the monster I have become. Getting out of bed is hard. Mirrors are avoided. I do not want to see the disgraced, guilty eyes of my reflection. When I do catch glimpses of myself, I look thin and hollow. I fear I might be starving to death.

I cross the street again and slip into a convenience store attached to a gas station. I throw a pack of gum on the front counter and wait for the pimple-faced kid behind the counter to punch the numbers into the ancient cash register. On my right is a small tower of various newspapers and there, on the front page, printed in bold is

The New Hampshire Vampire Killings. My heart thunders in my chest. I scan the other papers, and they are all titled similarly. *Vampire in New Hampshire. A Vampire Walks Among Us.*

I swipe one of the newspapers from the rack and add it to my purchase. The kid eyeballs it and sighs, returning to the register. Each time his finger strikes a key, my heart pumps a surge of adrenaline through my veins.

"You hear about this? It's some crazy shit." the kid says, referencing the newspaper. I ignore him, slap a five on the counter, and exit. I lean against the outside of the brick building with the newspaper clutched in my sweaty hand. After a deep breath, I skim the front page:

Police are still searching for the killer believed to be responsible for the deaths of six New Hampshire residents... New, shocking evidence suggests the perpetrator may actually be consuming the blood of his victims... FBI brought in after the discovery of the most recent victim, Matt Meyers... The twenty-nine-year-old was found outside a local bar with his throat torn open... Police are asking residents with any information to come forward... Everyone is wondering the same thing, what will the New Hampshire Vampire do next...

My eyes trace the word 'vampire' over and over. I, like most people, am familiar with the stories, the tales of Dracula and the series by Anne Rice. Although my circumstances are similar, I prefer to distance myself from that word. Why? Because those stories never end well. The vampire is always staked through the heart, their heads chopped off, and mouths filled with garlic. Sometimes for dramatic effect, they burn to death in front of sunny windows, or their bodies are lit on fire while the town watches in awe. I am hoping things will turn out better for me.

I did not choose this life, nor was I bitten. Sometimes I wonder if this affliction was passed on to me by my father. A silly thought, I know. The human part of me still believes I can be cured, that it has nothing to do with my genetics. That is why I cringe at the word vampire—it is uncurable—especially when the Other whispers that I can live forever if it continues to feed. I crumble the newspaper and toss it in a garbage can.

. . .

I sit across from my brother in a dimly lit restaurant. For the last five minutes, Fred has been looking at me like he is seeing a ghost. He orders us two beers and a plate of nachos to split. I do not bother voicing that I no longer eat nachos or most other types of food for that matter. Instead, I stare back at him, wondering when the disbelief will leave his face. We are interrupted by the waitress who plops two cold beers in front of us.

Fred takes a sip. "Hey," he says finally, a more appropriate greeting for when people first meet rather than ten minutes into a meal. "It's good to see you again. To be honest, I thought it would never happen."

I sip my beer too, feeling the rush of carbonation settle in my empty stomach. "I suppose I thought the same," I reply.

"If it weren't for Clarice—"

"I didn't realize you two kept in touch. She was my friend, you know," I say. The anger that reverberates off my voice is more than I intended.

Fred exhales a laugh. "Jeez. I didn't realize it mattered so much to you. I don't want you taking it the wrong way. It's not like I go out and get drinks with her. In fact, I've only talked to her twice since Mom died. Both times were to see if she knew where *you* were. I tried to find you for a long time, Billie."

"I'm sorry," I say, draining half my beer.

"What's the deal with you and her anyway?"

"Nothing." I shrug.

"I mean you guys were always tight, but it seems like things are different now."

The waitress returns setting down a pile of nachos between us. They are topped with the works: Pico de Gallo, guacamole, and sour cream. Fred tears away a cheesy chunk. I refrain, knowing it will only make me sick.

"I don't know. I haven't seen Clare in over ten years. It's nice to finally have her back. I don't want to ruin things. It's funny though, June always said she hoped we'd end up together, and lately, I find myself wishing the same."

Fred's smirk widens into a grin. He reaches across the table and gives me a playful punch in the shoulder. "That's my boy. She's a nice girl."

I smile too. The scene transports me back to childhood when I worshiped the ground Fred walked on. A cluster of emotion forms in the back of my throat. I drink more beer, hoping to wash it down, but the sensation remains as Fred talks me through the things I've missed in the last eleven years. He works in advertising and owns a house just outside of Wolfeboro. I am ecstatic to discover he is married but the even bigger news—his wife is pregnant. My big brother is going to be a father. The announcement nearly causes me to fall over with disbelief and excitement.

"I hate to bring it up when things are going so well," Fred says, "but I just can't understand why you left Wolfeboro. Look at all the things you've missed, Billie. You've never even met my wife." He sighs. "How could you have left me? I had no one. Mom was gone. We both don't know where our fathers are. And Frank, well, fuck him. I hope he burns in hell."

I slouch backward. The tone has shifted. I realize my hopes of rekindling any kind of a relationship with my brother will mean addressing the issue of my disappearance head-on, something I will never entirely be able to do. "I left because I had to," I say. "I couldn't take another minute in that town. I was bullied there, Frank beat the shit of out me there, and Mom died there. That place ruined me. I wanted to get as far away from it as I could. At the time, I didn't think about anyone but myself. I left you and Clarice. Maybe that was wrong. Maybe things would have been different if I had stayed. All I can say is sorry."

"Sorry?" he huffs. "You left me to deal with everything by myself. Do you know what they said about us? They accused you and me of murdering Mom. They had the fucking nerve to say Frank was innocent." He snorts.

I'm reminded of my altercation with Matt Meyers at The Woodline Pub. "*You probably raped her cold, dead corpse,*" he'd said right before I slit his throat.

"I know exactly what they say," I respond.

"It's a fucking joke," Fred says, plopping another glob of nachos into his mouth. "All of it. How could people even take Frank's side knowing he was such a pathetic asshole? How many times did he beat Mom senseless?" He pauses to wash down his nachos with a sip of beer. "I was at work when it happened. You weren't even home from school. Frank was there. I mean, he ran to the liquor store quick just before I let Clarice in. I don't know what happened after that. I guess he came home extra angry or something."

I shake my head. "Clarice? What do you mean you let her in?"

"She showed up right before I left for work. She was locked out of her house, forgot her key at home. It was

November and cold enough to freeze your tits off, so she needed somewhere warm to wait. She said her dad would be home from work in ten minutes. She kept asking me when I thought Frank would be back. I told her probably awhile since he tends to drive around after picking up booze. Drinking and driving, another Frank specialty."

"You never told me that."

"About Clarice? I never told anyone that. Why would I? She was there for literally ten minutes then left."

"You didn't tell the police?"

Fred shakes his head.

"She might have seen something, heard something. Maybe Mom and Frank arguing before it happened?"

"I doubt it."

"She could have been hurt."

"She made it home okay," Fred says. "I remember her mom and dad walked over after the cruisers and ambulance arrived. Her dad put a hand on my shoulder and asked me if I was okay. He said Clarice would've been there, but when they started walking over, she felt sick and went home."

"I just wish I'd known," I say. "Maybe if I'd known she'd been there—"

"You could've what, Billie? It makes no difference. Frank did what he did."

"I know, but I was the first person to find her. Maybe if I'd been earlier. If I hadn't stopped at the convenience store to get goddamn candy I could have—"

"What? Frank would've put a knife in you too," Fred says.

"Maybe," I say. "Frank wasn't even there when I got home from school. What I never understood is why he left when you were there for the liquor store only to come back home, do what he did, and leave again."

"Alibi," Fred says.

"He had an alibi for a total of five minutes. It doesn't take long to buy beer. After that, nobody saw him.

Fred shrugged. "Never said he was smart."

"Plus, if he was trying to create an alibi that would have been premeditated. Why would he go through the work of establishing an alibi only to leave a mess in the kitchen? He must have known he'd be the first one to be blamed."

"Maybe because he's a psycho, Billie. Do you really think that idiot thought anything through in his life?"

Or maybe because he didn't do it. Could that be true? And if Frank didn't do it, did that mean that I did? Was I really such a monster that I drank my mother's—

"Listen, I want to put all that in the past. I want to talk about the *now*. At least that's what my therapist says I should do." Fred chuckles.

Fred orders us another round of beers. On an empty stomach, I'm beginning to feel a buzz.

"You're not hungry?" Fred asks. "You haven't touched the nachos. They used to be your favorite. You need to eat something. You're looking too skinny these days."

The euphoria I felt from reconnecting with Fred is fading. I think of the newspapers, their headlines. I am sure the story is being broadcasted all over the radio and television. Fred must have heard about, what the press has dubbed, The New Hampshire Vampire Killings by now.

"Fred, there is something I need to tell you."

"Sure," he says. He leans forward in the booth, his attention centered on me.

"I have a… I don't know, I guess you could call it a problem. I get these cravings. These horrible cravings to drink—"

"Shit. I'm an idiot," Fred says, reaching across the table he slides my beer glass towards him. "I didn't realize."

I study the glass. "No, no, it's not that. It's just… sometimes I feel like I'm not entirely human." I pause, biting my lower lip. "Like maybe I'm some sort of vampire." My heart bounces in my chest like there are two tiny people using it as a trampoline.

Fred sighs. I brace myself, waiting for the backlash, the disgust. "I get it, Bill," he begins. "I'm only sorry I didn't see it sooner." He puts his hand on top of mine. "We can get you help. I can lend you some money in the meantime to get you by, that way you won't have to be a vampire. You won't need to suck from Darlene and Gus."

My eyes bore into the table. My attempt to confide in my brother has failed, not even he can imagine the dark things I am capable of. I had hoped he'd understand, that he would save me from myself like my mother had tried to do more than a decade ago. It was a foolish thought. Despite what Fred says, he will never understand why I had to stay away from him for eleven years, and why I must continue to stay away.

I am dangerous.

My thoughts return to the day I found my mother. Frank had not been home. He had walked in to find me in the kitchen with my dead mother at my feet. Had it just been to create an alibi? Had I stumbled upon the terrible aftermath of Frank's violence or had he really stumbled upon the aftermath of mine? And if I could do that to my own mother, my brother isn't safe.

I rise, my thighs connecting with the underside of the booth. "Bye, Fred," I say, moving for the front door.

"Billie," he calls after me. "What the hell? Where are you going?"

I bump into an older gentleman and apologize.

"Murderer," he says, or at least that is what I think he says. It is only after he repeats himself that I hear the words for what they truly are. Excuse me.

I heave open the front door. The twilight has transitioned into full dark. The streetlights light up as I make my way to the last person I may have in this world.

CHAPTER 24

Billie

"Billie?" Clare answers the door in black yoga pants and a loose-fitting ACDC tee shirt that hangs off one shoulder. Her hair is piled into a messy bun, a few loose strands dangle in her face. "Is everything okay?"

I nod.

She opens the door wider. "My apartment is a goddamn mess. I was rearranging my bookshelves. You have shit for timing."

My eyes dart to the mess of poetry collections and novels strewn across the living room floor.

"You look like shit," she says, ushering me inside. "What's going on? Are you sick?"

I shake my head.

"I just saw you a week ago. Why do you look like you've lost fifteen pounds? Are you eating?"

No! I'm not eating, I want to scream. "I went to see my brother," I say instead, ignoring her questions.

"How'd that go?"

"Might've been a mistake," I reply, although whether I am talking about seeing Fred or confiding in him, I'm not quite sure. "I'm just so damn tired and… hungry. I feel like I've hurt so many people. I make up these stupid rules, telling myself I'll never hurt a woman or a child. But I'm a horrible person. I—"

"You're just upset. You're talking nonsense," she says, taking my hand. "Come on, I'll fix you up." She leads me down the hall to her bedroom. "We can sit in here where there is less, well, stuff."

I pause in the doorway suddenly unsure if I should be here at all. What are my intentions for coming here? To tell her what I am. Is that something I really think she can handle? I already know how it will play out. At first, she'll laugh, thinking I'm making some stupid joke. Then, she'll freeze. She will say she understands, that she will always be my friend, as she excuses herself to the other room where she'll dial 911 and whisper frantically into the phone for help.

"Don't just stand there. Take a seat. You look so… rigid," Clare says, nudging me forward. "I'll be right back."

I do as told, settling at the end of her bed. It does not make me feel any less rigid though. Clare's room is painted a dark gray, the same shade clouds turn when it rains. The bedspread is a deep black, in fact, almost everything in her room is. Snippets of what look like song lyrics, book quotes or poetry (maybe a mixture of all three) are plastered to the far wall in an artistic collage. From the bed, I can make out only a few lines in the dim lighting. One catches my eye. *Doubting, dreaming dreams no mortal ever dared to dream before* is written in large calligraphy and attributed to Edgar Allen Poe. Who would have thought one line could be so beautiful? I search the collage for other verses. I want to read more of the words that clicked with Clare enough to copy down in sweeping cursive and display on her wall.

"Hey," she says. "Brought some snacks." She has a glass balanced in each hand and two bags of chips tucked under her arm.

My stomach lurches at the sight of food.

She smiles. "Might've crushed the chips a bit, but it's the thought that counts." She hands me a rocks glass filled with a clear liquid and ice. "Made you a drink."

With the first sip, the unmistakable flavor of agave resonates on my tongue. "Tequila?"

"That okay? I squeezed a little lime in there too."

"Perfect," I reply. "I was just admiring your wall."

"Thanks. It's kind of my thing. Poetry. Lyrics. They let you say things you normally might not. Art gives people courage." She glances at the tattoo marking the inside of her forearm.

"Is that why you got that?" I ask.

She shrugs. "Yeah."

"What does it mean: never forget who you really are?"

"Exactly what it says." She smiles, but her eyes betray her, depicting sadness instead of joy. "Sometimes we need a reminder of who we are, that includes the good but mostly the bad." She circles the outside of her glass with her finger. "Do you know what I mean?"

I nod. I know exactly what she means. Maybe we should get matching tattoos. I nearly explode into hysterical laughter.

"Now it's my turn," she says. "How'd you get those?" She points to my wrist.

I glance down at the faded scars across my left forearm. They are so tiny I often forget I have them. They are like tally marks carved into flesh, each symbolizing a moment of weakness. A moment where I had let the Other win, fattening its stomach and its confidence with my blood. "I fell off my bike when I was younger. It was a bad fall. I slid into a barbed wire fence by one of the chicken farms."

Clare grimaces. Her fingers reach out and caress the exposed skin. "That must have hurt."

I envision my younger self taking a razor blade to the tender flesh, using it to get to what the Other needed beneath.

Clare tears open one of the chip bags, pops a few in her mouth, then extends the bag to me.

Another lurch in my gut. "No thanks."

"I thought you said you were hungry?"

"Not for chips."

She frowns, placing the bag on the bureau behind her. Tossing her head back, she swallows the rest of her drink. I study my glass a moment before doing the same. The tequila burns the back of my throat. At the same time, it makes me feel alive.

"Cheers," she says, raising her empty glass.

I return the gesture with a smile. "I think the cheers is supposed to come first."

She giggles. "Seriously though, I'm proud of you for seeing your brother. I know that was probably difficult."

I sigh. "I'm not sure if I'll see him again. He can't understand why I left Wolfeboro."

"People have different reactions to things, Billie. That doesn't make one person right or wrong. Sometimes, the most important thing you can do is look after yourself."

"Either way, I'm not sure he will ever understand the person I've become."

"Well, it's a good thing I do then."

I half-smile. For a moment, I think about confiding in her. Maybe she would… could understand. Then, I am reminded of my brother's reaction. His innocent ignorance. I would really have to spell it out, explain in gruesome detail what I have done, what the Other makes me do. It would be messy. There would be too many questions, too many looks of horror.

Clare bounces to a stand and runs out of the room. I hear the quick patter of her feet as she scurries to the kitchen and back where she practically dives onto the bed with laughter.

"The cure to everything," she says between heavy breaths while holding up a bottle of tequila.

"I'd like to see your sources on that because I have a feeling there are a lot of people that may disagree. Some that might even claim tequila is responsible for a lot of their problems."

"Well, screw them." She pours two more drinks. We gulp them down in unison.

I see the alcohol's effect mirrored in her eyes. Not the dead, vacant stare of drunk, but the glittery look of someone having a good time. Those blue eyes of hers are so damn beautiful. I swallow hard, returning to the rigid posture I'd arrived with.

"Well," she says, "If there is one thing we have gained from all this, it's each other."

Before I can respond, she kisses me. It is a deep kiss that sends a shiver down my spine. She breaks away, studying my reaction. Her blue eyes glisten with excitement, and her lips curve into a soft smile. I do not want to imagine what she sees in my eyes. Is it the distant, cold look of a killer, or the inhuman look of a monster?

She kisses me again nearly causing me to gasp in surprise. The kiss is harder, her tongue finding its way into my mouth. I reach for her thigh, and she swings her leg over me using my shoulders as leverage. My fingers find the edge of her shirt and brush the soft skin of her lower back. I stiffen. God, I want her. Do I dare slide my hands higher?

She leans back and pulls off her shirt, my question answered. A black lace bra shows off the swell of her breasts. I take in the smell of her. The raspberry shampoo in her hair, the soft scent of vanilla on her skin, the faint odor of tequila from her breath. I want to see what is under that bra and she shows me, revealing herself with a quick unhinge of the bra's clasp.

She shoves me backward, and I collapse onto the bed. When I peer up, I glimpse her bare breasts in the dim light and grow stiffer. Tugging at our clothes, we become entangled in the sheets. Then, somehow, I am entering her. It is everything I have ever wanted since I was sixteen and old enough to know that I wanted *her*. She begins kissing my cheek, my chest, my neck. I freeze as her lips linger over my throat, her kisses turning into delicate sucking.

Not there.

She will wake *it*.

It's not her fault. She does not realize what she is doing. I bring my hands to the base of her neck. It is my intention to redirect her lips back to mine. Instead, my hand hovers above her throat. The Other peeks its head. Suddenly I can hear her heartbeat, see the light pulsing of her jugular. My mouth aches. Would her blood taste like warm vanilla and raspberry? A spasm shoots into my groin.

Clare's mouth returns to mine. I shake my head. "No," I mutter.

She stops. "What?" Her brow wrinkles in concern.

"This isn't… we can't… do this," I pant.

"But don't you think this feels right? That we are supposed to…"

It does feel right. Of course, it does. I want nothing more than to hold her hand while I explain this whole awful mess to her. I want to stay up late drinking tequila, laughing, and snuggling under the blankets with her until dawn. But her face is hovering only a few inches from mine, her throat still pulsing in my ear. Couldn't she hear that? God, it is deafening. My jaw clicks. The Other yearns. How long would it take for me to sink my teeth into her throat?

I grab her waist and flip her onto her back, pulling out from inside her. We switch positions in seconds, me now straddling her, pinning her arms above her head. She lets out a gasp. Not out of fear as it should have been but out of surprise, maybe even excitement.

I am stronger than her. It would only take a second to lean down and…

I push myself off her. The bedsprings creak from the release of my weight. I do not look back as I charge out of her bedroom. I throw on my wrinkled clothes and sprint from her apartment into the cool night air. It is clear as I turn the corner that the Other is back, and it demands to be fed.

CHAPTER 25

Eleven Years Ago

Less than twenty-four hours after his mother's death, the police ushered Bill into a cold, sterile room. It was the kind of room you saw on television shows like *Law and Order* and *Criminal Minds*. Bill had expected kinder treatment. After all, his mother had just been killed, and he had discovered her mutilated body. He wished the room was painted a bright blue and filled with toys, books, and stuffed animals. He hoped a plump woman named Susan would step around the corner, introduce herself in a sing-song voice, and envelope him in a hug. Instead, he was greeted by a stern-looking man who introduced himself as Detective Lounds. The detective had such a cold penetrating gaze, Bill suspected he could have made Stonewall Jackson shake in his boots.

"Take a seat, Mr. Dunne," Lounds said.

Bill did, plopping down with such force the metal chair rattled against the tile floor. The detective began with a rehearsed sorry-for-your-loss bit. Bill just nodded.

"William, walk me through your day on November 17th." The detective addressed him more like a man than a kid which, at eighteen, was probably how he should be spoken to. None the less, Bill didn't like him.

"It's Billie," he responded.

Lounds narrowed his eyes. "Okay, Billie. Please, start from the beginning. What did you do that morning?"

"I went to school."

"What time did you wake up?"

"I always set my alarm for 7:00 a.m. School starts at 8:20."

Lounds made a quick notation on a legal pad. "Okay, continue."

"I went to school," he said again. This time he wanted to yell it. It was stupid to force people into stale, white interview rooms like this. It made you feel guilty, even if you weren't, which in return made you feel hostile. Rooms like this caused everything that came out of your mouth to sound like a lie, not that the police cared. Sometimes they were so preoccupied with finding someone to blame, they condemned the innocent.

"Where was your mother?"

"My mother?" Tears threatened to explode out of him. He held them back, his throat sore from the effort. "She was asleep. She worked a late shift at the bar. She always makes me lunch when she gets home. So, I grabbed it from the fridge and left around 8:00."

"How did you get to school that morning?"

"I walked like I always do. The school's about fifteen minutes from my house, ten if I walk fast."

"And you remained in the building until your dismissal at…" Lounds paused to reference his notepad, "2:20 p.m.?"

"Yes."

"What time did you return home from school?"

"I don't know, maybe 3:00. I stopped at the convenience store for some candy." Kit Kats and Musketeers to be precise. He could still taste the chocolate and caramel in his mouth when he had found her. The sweetness had turned rotten.

"What happened when you arrived at your house?"

Suddenly his heart was beating too fast. Bill slid his chair back, the legs squeaking horribly. He had the wild idea that if he bolted for the door he could escape. Maybe if he ran fast enough, he could dodge all the police and Detective Lounds and never have to think about any of this ever again.

"Her car was in the driveway," Bill began. "The trunk was open and filled with groceries like she was in the middle of unloading it. I grabbed a few bags to bring inside and… right away… I… I… knew something was wrong." He paused to take a deep breath. "Some groceries had spilled. A bunch of grapes had rolled into the living room." Those grapes had been everywhere. Fat little green grenades waiting to explode under the weight of his sneaker. "I went into the kitchen, and I found her." He didn't tell Lounds how he had fallen to his knees and screamed her name. Nor did he explain how he'd leaned over her and whispered *rose petals*, praying she would sit up laughing like it was some sort of sick joke. April Fools in November.

"I'm sorry, son. That's not an easy thing."

Bill wanted him to shut up. The detective's condolences did not help. They weren't sincere, and it certainly would not bring his mother back.

"Did you call an ambulance?"

"No," he responded. At the time, the thought to call for help hadn't even crossed his mind. He knew she was already dead. There was so much blood and, oddly, the *feeling* of no life, no soul. He had plenty of practice watching life leave the cats he fed off. He was more than familiar with what death felt like. "Frank did."

Lounds raised a thick eyebrow. "For the record, we are talking about Frank Dunne, your stepfather?"

"Yes."

"So, Frank called the ambulance? When did your stepfather arrive home?" The detective asked each question with a dead, emotionless tone as if he was reading items off a menu.

"I don't know. I don't remember."

"You don't remember?"

"No." The last thing he remembered, in fact, was Frank shaking him. *Billie, what's going on? What's wrong with your mother?* Then, his stepfather was screaming, kneeling in her blood, caressing her hair. *What have you done, Billie? What the fuck have you done?*

"Where had Frank been?" Lounds asked.

"I don't know where he was. Did you ask my brother? He might know," Bill said. He stared straight ahead, over Detective Lounds' shoulder. It was easier than looking him in the eye. If he did that, Bill suspected he would start crying.

"Someone is speaking to your brother right now," the detective said while scribbling notes on his legal pad. "Your brother claims he was at your house for a few hours before leaving for work that afternoon. Can you confirm that?"

Bill shook his head. "I was at school. Fred moved out awhile back. He stops by a lot though. Mostly to steal food from the fridge. Sometimes to see me and Mom."

"Why did Fred move out?"

"Probably to get away from Frank. He's old enough. He'll be twenty-five in a few months."

"Do you know your stepfather to be capable of violence?"

"Yes," Bill responded, but the detective must already know that answer. By now, he would have seen the police reports. Bill would need to use all his fingers and some toes to count the number of times the cops had been called on his stepfather. It was usually the neighbors. The police would show up and slap labels on his family's dysfunction: disorderly conduct, disturbing the peace, assault. Misdemeanors and infractions punished with fines instead of serious action. Most of the time nothing happened. No matter how hard she was hit, his mother never ratted Frank out. It always came down to her "clumsiness". Oh, she just walked into a door again. Oops, she just fell down the stairs for the third time this year. It is nearly impossible to prosecute an abuser without the victim's cooperation. Another ridiculous loophole in the legal system.

"Was he ever violent with you?"

"Yes," Bill said, his eyes still trained on the wall behind Detective Lounds.

"Did Frank ever hit your brother?"

"Yes. He hit all of us," Bill said, "but mostly my mother." The statement summoned unwelcomed images: his mother taking a fist to the face, Frank grabbing her by the throat as Bill pounded on his back to let her go. Hot tears welled in his eyes. His mother had taken the worst of it. Bill and his brother had only been in the way. Their beatings were simply to supplement the rage Frank felt for their mother. He thought of his stepfather crying over her body. The pain had looked real but were they only crocodile tears? *Billie, what have you done? What the fuck have you done?*

"I always knew he'd do it," Bill said.

"And what's that?" Lounds asked.

"I always knew one day he'd kill her."

CHAPTER 26

Clare

My second trip to Wolfeboro is a more enjoyable experience. For one, I do not have Billie practically shitting his pants from anxiety next to me, nor do I have to face the drama of a funeral. Still, I cannot shake the uneasiness I feel growing inside me like a fetus in a womb.

I have replayed the incident with Billie in my bedroom over and over, searching for where I went wrong. Did I come on too strong? Should I have waited to make a move? Maybe it was just the visit with his brother that had upset him. God knows everyone is on edge lately with news of a killer running loose. Yet, something tells me it was none of those things. After all, it is not every day a guy bolts from a woman's room. Men don't typically do that sort of thing, especially in the middle of sex.

My throat constricts as I pass Billie's old house. It is such a simple structure from the outside, even painted a bland white. It is hard to imagine the horrors that have taken place inside. I have yet to meet the new owners, a young couple with a Labrador, but I hope to God they smudged the living hell out of that place, too much bad juju there.

My mother whips open the front door. "Clarice," she squeals. "It's such a rare pleasure to see my baby twice in one week. Please tell me you're staying for a bit. I'll put on some tea."

I place my keys on the front hall table. "Sounds great, Mom."

"I'm happy you're picking up that bin of old poetry. The more clutter I can cleanse this house of the better." My mother bustles into the kitchen. The banging of cabinets is followed by the faint click of the gas burner catching. "Maybe I'll throw together a quick cheese plate too. Are you hungry?"

I roll my eyes, knowing it will take a while. My mother will spend an extra ten minutes ensuring each slice of cheese is even and squared off into perfect ninety-degree angles. It is the perfectionist in her.

"Sure. I'll go grab that stuff now. I'll just be a minute."

Upstairs, I open my closet and remove the poetry bin. I place the box on the bed and peer inside. The notebooks are piled hastily on top of each other just as I'd left them. The book of darkness rests on top. I resist the urge to flip through it and refasten the lid.

As I turn to leave, I notice a folded letter on crisp, white stationery sitting on my bureau. Next to it lies a torn envelop, the nest I assume the note was birthed from. *What in the world?* I set the bin down, my fingers fidgeting by my side. Someone has already read the letter. My mother, I assume. "Why are you opening my mail, Mother?" I shout.

I hear her hurried footsteps on the stairs, the creak of the seventh step. "What's that, honey?"

I ignore her, unfolding the note.

Clarice, I've been reading the newspapers. I know who the New Hampshire Vampire is. I think you'll want to know too.

That's it. No signature. Just three sentences handwritten, a blank white page surrounding them. Why would I care about the New Hampshire Vampire? Who would even be sending mail to my parents' house? Everyone important to me knows I live in Concord now.

My stomach performs a massive flip flop. There is something about this note I do not like. My eyes fall to the torn envelope. I flip it over. 'Berlin Federal Correctional Institution' is stamped in the left-hand corner. Suddenly the envelope feels unclean. I let it fall to the ground as if it is toxic waste and rub my sweaty palms on my jeans.

"Clarice?" my mother says from the doorway. Her voice reminds me of a child who has been caught with their hand in the cookie jar before dinner. "I didn't mean for you to see that. At least not today."

I turn to face her. "Why are you opening my mail?"

"I saw who it was from and, well, I wanted to know why *he* was writing you." Her fingers swirl between each other in an unspoken argument. "I mean, why in the fuck is Frank writing you?"

I flinch at her rising tone and her use of *fuck*. My mother never swears.

"What does he mean?" she asks, her manicured finger pointing to the letter at my feet.

"I don't know," I mutter.

"What do you mean you don't know?" She is screaming now, her face a light pink. "After all these years, he just randomly decides to write to you. Has he sent you letters before?"

I shake my head.

"And what's all this about the New Hampshire Vampire? What in the world does that have to do with you?"

"I don't know!" I scream back, matching her octave, my voice betraying just as much anxiety.

She takes a step back.

"Listen, Mom, I'm going to tell you something... something... I don't like to talk about."

She nods. "Of course. You know you can tell me anything."

I take a deep breath, attempting to slow my pounding heart. "The summer before high school Frank raped me."

My mother gasps, her hands flutter to her mouth. "No," she whispers.

"I was at Billie's one night watching a movie. His mom offered for Frank to drive me home because it was late. When we got here, Frank put the car in park and locked the doors. He was really drunk. I was only fourteen. I was terrified. He told me if I screamed, he'd kill you and Dad. I believed him too. The worst part of it all was that we were right outside this house. I mean, I could see the TV through the curtains. I knew you and Dad were just on the other side of that wall, and there was nothing you could do to stop him."

"Oh my God, Clarice." She leans against the wall, steadying herself. Her face is stark white, for one horrifying second, I think she might faint. "I had no idea. If I knew... if I knew... I'd fucking kill him. We could've gone to court. We—"

"I know."

"Why didn't you tell me?" she asks, her eyes dripping hot tears, smudging her mascara. "You know you can tell me anything."

"I told Dad."

"Wha—what?"

"I told Dad maybe a month after it happened. He called me a liar."

"Why would he say that?" she wept.

I shake my head. Tears sting my eyes. "At first, I couldn't understand why he didn't go running over there like dads are supposed to do. Why he didn't hold a knife to Frank's fat throat and make him beg for his life. Then, I realized Dad was just as afraid of Frank as I was. It was easier for him to think I lied than for him to confront that drunk asshole."

"That's not a good reason. He could've called the police, he could've—"

"He told me Frank was the type of crazy a man didn't want to mess with. He said not even the Law could hold him." I exhale a laugh. "Funny how things turn out."

My mother rushes forward and surrounds me in a tight hug. "I'd wish you told me," she murmurs over and over.

After a minute, I push her away. My mind decided. "I'm going to see him," I say.

"No. No, you are not."

I strut towards the door.

My mother catches my wrist. "What is wrong with you, Clarice? Why would you go to Berlin?"

"Because I don't want to let what Frank did to me waste a second more of my life," I say. "After that night, I stopped hanging out with Billie, my best friend. I would cry and pray I could regain what that prick took from me. I've wasted too many years of my life on what Frank's actions set in motion. Everything is his fault. I am done avoiding it. I am done crying. It has been fifteen fucking years. I am not afraid of him anymore." I grab the bin of poetry and sprint down the stairs with the harsh click-clack of my mother's heels on the wooden steps behind me.

"Clarice? Clarice?" she cries.

I scoop up my keys from the hall table and yank the front door open.

"Maybe that note isn't even real," she suggests. "Maybe it's just a sick joke, some kids who knew Billie had been in town." She pauses to catch her breath. "When you brought Billie back to Wolfeboro it caused quite a ruckus. You know what people say about him. What they think he did."

"I know," I say, continuing down the steps. "Once again, the victim is prosecuted. People rarely see the truth, and when they finally do, they never believe it. They all suck!"

She chases after me. "Clarice, please."

I force open my car door, toss the poetry bin in the back, and slide onto the leather seat. When I go to shut the door, my mother catches it.

"Can I just ask how many times it happened? How many times Frank did that to you?"

"It only happened once," I respond. "But that's all it takes." She steps aside defeated, and I slam the door shut.

As I throw the car in reverse, I remember the promise I made after it happened. Even at fourteen, I knew I'd kill Frank or any man if they ever tried to do that to me again.

CHAPTER 27

Clare

My hands tighten on the steering wheel as I take the exit for Berlin Correctional Institution. I pull into the parking lot with little on my mind other than getting the information I need.

"Is the inmate expecting you?" the pinched faced secretary asks from behind a small cut out in the plastic cell surrounding her.

"He damn well should be," I respond.

I am stripped of my purse and cellphone, buzzed through door after door, sign the forms that need to be signed, until finally, I am directed to the visitation room. It is nothing short of what you see in movies. Two parallel counters span the entirety of the room, a thick divider separating them. A small wall extends every few feet designating not-so-private-cubbies. Each cubby is equipped with opposing chairs and phones.

A guard directs me to the far cubicle. I sit obediently with my hands clenched in my lap. A door opens, and Frank appears. His eyes lock onto mine from across the room. He holds my gaze as he is escorted to the chair opposite me. The guards plop him down. He smiles and picks up the phone. I do the same.

"Clarice, you look different," Frank says.

A shiver travels up my spine. He looks different too. A whole lot better actually. Maybe this is exactly what he needed, a twelve-year-long detox. His hair has thinned and grayed, but he must have lost at least thirty pounds of excess beer gut.

"I'm sorry about your grandmother," he says.

"How did you know about that?" I demand, heat rushing to my face. I do not want his eyes on me. Suddenly, I feel like he has been watching me all these years, hiding in bushes and peering through windows.

"Like I said in my letter… I read the paper."

I nearly breathe out a sigh of relief. My crawling skin settles the slightest bit.

"Thank you for coming."

"I'm only here because you are behind that glass."

"It's plastic actually," he chuckles, rapping it with his knuckles. "Everything is nowadays."

"Enough small talk. Why did you write me? What is it you think you know?" I ask.

"Ah, a woman that gets right to the point. I like that." He smirks. "I've kept my mouth shut about this for far too long. Don't know why. That little shit certainly had no problem throwing me under the bus."

"Just tell me what you have to say."

"Billie is the New Hampshire Vampire," he whispers.

Now, it's my turn to laugh. "This is why you dragged me down here? To tell me lies. I'm sure it gets lonely in here, but are you really that desperate for visitors?" I remove the phone from my ear. As I go to holster it, Frank's meaty hand bangs on the divider so loudly it causes me to jump. The officer in the far corner advances, a finger pointed in accusation at Frank. Frank brushes him off, mouthing an apology I cannot hear.

I return the phone to my ear. "All right. Prove it then," I challenge.

"When Billie was fifteen, I woke up to the sound of him moving around the house," Frank begins. "I'd passed out in the bathroom. I heard some noise in the kitchen, figured he was just up getting a glass of water. But then, I heard the backslider open. I thought that little shit was sneaking out. To go where? Hell, I don't know. He had no friends. I went into my bedroom and looked out the window facing the backyard." He pauses. "The kid was crouched in the grass drinking the blood of a goddamn cat."

I shake my head. "You must have been mistaken. Drunk. Hallucinating."

He shakes his head. "I know what I saw, and I know exactly where all those missing neighborhood cats went. Remember those few months? Handmade posters taped to telephone poles: 'Missing Cat. Reward $200.' Of course, it continued beyond those few months. That little asshole just got smarter, looked outside the neighborhood."

A flicker of a memory presents itself. Running into Billie one night. I was drunk. A party at Brett's. When I asked Billie what he was doing, he said he was looking for his cat. I shake my head. "And you think Billie was behind that missing cat business?"

"Cats are easy prey. They get let outside. Nobody's watching them. People just hope they'll come back at night. When they don't, oh well, parents just get a new one to appease their snot-nosed kids."

"That doesn't prove anything. It's circumstantial."

Frank snorts. "Those recent murders, I bet if you looked at where the bodies were found, Billie was in those towns at the same time. Like the cats, he moves on to the next place before anyone gets suspicious. Same hunt, bigger game."

My mind sorts through all the information I know about the New Hampshire Vampire Killings. The first body had been found in Barren where Billie currently lives. The most recent had been discovered right behind Carl's Diner the day after he had been there with me. Spots flash before my eyes and, if I had not already been sitting, I might have fallen. If I went back over the earlier murders the police had linked to the New Hampshire Vampire, would I find Billie had also been in those towns? Is Frank right? It's impossible.

I shrug. "Coincidence."

"Coincidence my ass," Frank replies. "Look, I wish I was wrong, but all I have in here is time to think."

"Why should I believe anything *you* say?"

"Why did you come here in the first place, Clarice? Maybe because there is a part of you that knows Billie isn't right. That he's dangerous. Sick."

"I... I... came—"

"I have no reason to lie to you. Not while I'm in here."

"What makes you think I'm even still in touch with Billie? He hasn't been back to Wolfeboro in eleven years."

"*Tsk. Tsk.* How many times do I have to tell you I read the paper?" He reaches beneath the shelf in front of him revealing a newspaper. He thumbs to the third page then holds it to the glass. "June was the founder of the Wolfeboro Veterans Society. When people like that pass, their deaths don't go unnoticed."

'June Gold, Founder of the WVS, Dies at Eighty-six' headlines the paper. The black and white picture depicts a scene from the funeral, and there, in the center of the crowd, is me in my black dress with Billie by my side.

"Why are you telling me this? Why not Fred?"

Frank places the newspaper back beneath the shelf. "Fred is a useless prick. He sees me as the enemy. He will just defend his brother, probably help him dig the graves of his victims if Billie asks. But I had hoped you would be different, that you would believe me."

"And what makes you think that I wouldn't also see you as the enemy?"

"Fine. If you won't take my word, take Billie's mothers. My Eve knew about the cats. She'd seen it herself once. She talked him into seeing a therapist, and they blew through them one by one, always searching for a second opinion, always hoping for another diagnosis. Conduct Disorder. That's what they all said. Do you know what that is, Clarice?"

I shake my head.

"That's code word for he's a damn psycho. The beginning ingredients for a sociopath, 'course that's not what the doctors are calling it nowadays. Billie's mother, Eve, she swore the doctors were wrong. '*He's a good boy,*' she'd say, '*he stays out of trouble. He knows the difference between right and wrong.*' And this may blow your socks off, but I agreed with her. Billie has empathy, that's what made him such a pussy. It was the aggression towards animals the psychiatrists were puzzled by. Finally, when he was a little older, a young doctor with new-age ideas whispered Renfield Syndrome in Eve's ear."

"What is this Renfield Syndrome?"

"I don't know, some vampire mumbo jumbo. Whatever it was, it scared the shit right out of Eve."

"I'm not sure if I believe you. I've never heard of it."

"Did you ever see any scars on him?"

The tiny slashes on Billie's wrists pop into my mind. I nod. "He told me they were from a bad fall on his bike. He slid into a barbed-wire fence."

Frank snorts. "That's how that shit starts. Something happens that gives them a hankering for blood. They cut themselves to get more. When that doesn't work, they usually look for animals. When they tire of that, well, you know what I'm getting at."

"Billie isn't a murderer, that's you. Are you forgetting that you killed your wife?"

Frank's face turns a splotchy red. "I did *not* kill my wife. I loved her."

"You loved her? Really? Is that why you hit her every day? Is that why you abused her sons?" I hinge forward, my face only a few inches from the fingerprint ridden plastic separating us. "Is that why you raped me?"

He sighs. "That was wrong. I know that now. I've had a lot of time to think in this dump. But don't start crying rape." His voice drops to a whisper. "It's been fifteen years, sweetheart. No one will believe you anyway. It's frustrating when nobody believes you, take my word for it."

I snort a laugh.

Frank leans forward, meeting my gaze. "I'm a lot of things, Clarice, but I am not a murderer. If you want to know who killed my Eve, you might want to talk to Billie about that."

"You think Billie killed his own mother?"

Franks nods. "I don't just know it, I am positive. The more Eve researched this Renfield Syndrome, the more she wanted Billie to get help. She wanted to send him away, but he was eighteen by then, so she needed him to commit himself. I have a feeling the day she died was the same day she confronted that little shit about it." His voice falls to an even lower whisper. "He'd rather kill his mother than stop drinking blood. Think on that."

"You're sick, Frank. You're a rapist. A murderer. The worst of the worst," I say.

"I am not a murderer!" he screams and slams his fist into the divider.

I jump, the phone almost slipping from my hand. Two cops move towards him.

"Vampires aren't just scary stories, Clarice. They can be real." The phone falls from his hand as the officers seize him by the arms and hoist him to a stand. Before they vanish beyond the locked door, Frank glances back at me. Our eyes lock and, in that moment, I know I have misjudged him. Frank may be a good for nothing liar, but he is not lying about this. Why would he bother?

CHAPTER 28

Clare

I leave the prison with shaky legs and trembling hands. I hop back into my Subaru without the faintest idea of where to go. I could return to my mother's house, but the thought of her restless hands and tearful eyes gives me second thoughts. Should I drive to Barren and confront Billie? No, that's something I am not prepared for. Despite Frank's apparent sincerity, there's a chance he is attention-seeking. Just because he and Billie's mother thought they saw something does not make it true. A lot of people spot UFO's in the sky every day too, that doesn't mean the FBI should open a real-life *X Files* department.

Maybe I should call Fred and tell him what nonsense Frank is spouting. I remove my cellphone and stare at the black screen. He was making some crazy accusations. Vampires. Psychiatrists. Dead Cats. Frank's an idiot, but his insistence is unnerving. I tap my phone screen, bringing it to life, and pull up Google. I type Renfield Syndrome in the search bar. What I discover is almost enough for me to power off my phone.

Renfield Syndrome, also known as Clinical Vampirism, is a psychological disorder not currently recognized by the DSM (basically the bible of psychology) although there appears to be some research to back it up. The syndrome is named after Renfield, Dracula's obsessive follower in Bram Stoker's novel.

The condition starts in childhood after an incident causes the child to associate blood with excitement or pleasure. Since the disorder is not formally recognized, there is some conflicting information on the exact symptoms. However, most articles say by adolescence, sufferers of Clinical Vampirism graduate to consuming their own blood, also known as auto vampirism. I lift my head, reminded of those scars on Billie's wrist. Were they really from a barbed-wire fence?

My phone rings, causing me to flinch. My mother is calling. Not now, I can't deal with her now. I decline the call sending her to voicemail. I resume my research. Clicking into article after article, I pray one will disprove Frank's theory. Instead, they only help to clarify it. Sometimes, after auto vampirism, people will go on to consuming the blood of animals. My mind races with memories of those missing cats. I remember those posters Frank mentioned. Homemade signs created by children that promised rewards for bringing home their beloved pet. My stomach drops.

My phone indicates a new voicemail. I ignore it and continue reading. The next step of the disorder is to ingest the blood of other humans. This is often done between consenting adults, however, in rare cases, blood can be obtained through violence. Drinking blood from other humans comes with obvious risks such as disease. Maybe that's why Billie looks so sickly. Did he catch some sort of illness? Or maybe, he is so far gone that he's living almost entirely off blood. Now that I think of it, I've barely seen Billie touch actual food. Sure, a few slices of pot roast here and there, but is that enough to sustain a grown man? Of course not. He probably has a severe vitamin deficiency. Billie could actually be dying.

No. No. No. This is ludicrous. Billie does not have Renfield Syndrome. Surely, I would have noticed all this happening when we were kids, teenagers. It's coincidental. Frank is trying to scare me. Once a bully always a bully.

Maybe there were signs though. The missing cats being the biggest. What did Frank say about the New Hampshire Vampire murders? Same game, bigger prey.

I've had enough. I close the tab with trembling hands. My phone flashes reminding me of the voicemail from my mother. I take a deep breath and play it:

Clarice, it's Mom. I know you think I'm calling to talk about what happened earlier, but I'm not. I... I... just wanted to let you know that Matt Myers is dead. They discovered his body in the woods not far from The Woodline Pub. I know you went to school with him and figured you'd want to know. It made the papers this afternoon. They think it may be linked to the New Hampshire Vampire. I was wondering if that's what Frank was trying to—

I end the message, my heart pounding. I pull out of Berlin Federal Correctional Institution and merge onto the highway. My mind is full of racing thoughts and blank at the same time. It is a cold, numb feeling.

I take the exit towards Concord. That is when it really hits me. Billie *is* the New Hampshire Vampire. The evidence is too damning. Shaking my head, I force the idea away and try to focus on the road. Suddenly, it is too dark. I am too alone. The winding pavement is treacherous. The country roads, I know like the back of my hand, seem foreign. The houses farther apart. The forest thicker. Anything could be lurking in these woods: bears, a madman, a pack of wolves. I would be oblivious to their presence just as I had been oblivious to the fact that Billie is... is... what?

Say it.

"A murderer," I whisper to the empty car. Frank was right. I have the urge to scream. I hold it in, swallowing the rock in my throat. The only thing keeping me sane is the friendly glow from the homes I pass. The simple reminder that normally exists for others. Maybe not for me, but for the families huddled around televisions and dinner tables.

I make the decision then to confront Billie in the morning. He deserves to hear it from me before I consider taking this information to the police. He is my best friend, after all. I love him.

I will practice what I'll say to him tonight. I must stop him from hurting any more people. My hands tighten around the steering wheel. I have to stop him. It has to work. I focus on this new mantra, trying to ignore the fact that the houses are diminishing as I drive deeper into the New Hampshire woods. It is only when a light switches off in the distance that I begin to scream.

PART IV
INSATIABLE

CHAPTER 29

Billie

I am too weak. The duality of my nature is exhausting. The human part of me wants to keep pushing, encouraged by the hopeless belief that I can break myself of this affliction. It's a stupid fairytale I have told myself since the day Frank broke my nose and blood leaked into my throat. But the Other continues to whisper that there is no cure, that I am exactly what the newspapers are calling me—a vampire.

After my conversation with Fred and the horrible accusation Matt Myers made before his death, I am certain I killed my mother. It makes sense. I was the first one home that day. Frank had been at the liquor store. Would he really come home, kill his wife, then leave again? Maybe he would if it meant taking the attention off him. If that was the case, why would he leave such a horrid scene in the kitchen? Why wouldn't he set up a shatterproof alibi? He must have known the police would suspect him, the abusive husband. It was always the husband.

He could have covered it up, cleaned the crime scene, hidden evidence. Because he did none of those things, it makes more sense that it was me. My cravings got out of hand, the Other demanded blood, and it found some. The act was so traumatizing, the human part of me dissociated.

No. No. That isn't right. I couldn't have done that to my mother. I would remember. I was at school. People saw me. But both Frank and I's fingerprints were all over that kitchen. If I didn't do it, why had Frank screamed and cried, *"What have you done, Billie?"* Why would he say that?

I cannot think. My thoughts are racing. I pace my tiny room, catching sight of myself in the small mirror above the dresser. My eyes are sunken and outlined by a blackish-purple ring. I am too thin. My skin is so pale in the fluorescent light it appears a pale blue. When I stare at my reflection, I already see a corpse. Maybe I am the living dead, or maybe this is my last and only chance to save myself.

After much deliberation, I know what needs to be done. I need to feed, but not just on any blood—the blood of the innocent. Blood that is untainted by antidepressants, alcohol, late-night fast food runs, and the hardships of adult life. I need a pure life force. The Other desires a child, and I know exactly where to get one.

* * *

As predicted, the backdoor is unlocked. They usually are in these country homes. I slip into the quiet house and disappear among the shadows. I am careful to maneuver around obstacles, attempting to recall the house's layout from my brief visit after June's funeral. I creep upstairs to the lilac painted room. I pause in the doorway, listening for signs of movement from the parents' bedroom. The house is still.

I hover above the toddler's bed. My chance to walk away has long passed. The rational part of my brain has been overrun by panic, hunger, and the fear of death. I scoop the toddler into my arms with the gentleness of a mother. She lets out a soft sigh but remains asleep. I turn around to find a child standing in the doorway.

She rubs her eyes. "What are you doing?"

I recall the little girl from the funeral reception. She had been sitting with her knees drawn to her chest, and a pink iPod glued to her face. Now, she is in pajamas adorned with puppies. It is Erin's other daughter, the toddler's big sister.

"Go back to sleep," I say. I flirt with the idea of adding *this is only a dream* but resist the Freddy Krueger cliché. Children are smarter than most adults think. They know the difference between sincerity and bullshit. I am at her mercy. If she screams, I am dead.

"What are you doing with my sister?" she asks.

"I need your sister, so I can live," I respond. "You do want me to live, don't you?"

The girl nods.

"Then go back to bed," I urge.

"Are you a bad guy?" she asks.

I sigh, giving the question some thought. "I like to think I'm not."

The girl studies me a moment then turns and pads down the hall back to her room.

I hold my breath. When I hear her bedroom door creak shut, I move. My confidence wavers as I pass the parent's room. I picture the mother opening the door and screaming. The father stumbling out asking me *what in the hell do I think I'm doing,* right before he bludgeons me to death with the baseball bat he keeps by his bedside. Despite my fears, none of this happens. I retrace my steps until I am back outside.

I run to my car. The child's head bounces with each step, and she lets out a soft cry. I hush her back to sleep and lie her across the backseat of my Toyota. I dash around to the driver's side door and peer up at the house. The upstairs' light flicks on.

CHAPTER 30

Eleven Years Ago

Billie sat on a bench in the hallway of the police station with his hands folded in his lap. Police officers passed periodically, but nobody paid him any attention. It was just like high school. He was invisible, forgotten. Eventually, his brother, finished with his interrogation, came out and joined him.

"What did they ask you?" Fred inquired.

Bill shrugged.

"What did you tell them?"

"The truth," Bill responded.

They sat there for what felt like hours, neither one of them sure of how to proceed. Heck, they weren't even clear on whether they could legally leave or not. Frank was still being interviewed somewhere within the belly of the station.

The chaos and confusion had been physically draining. Bill wanted to take a nap, but he did not want to go home. If he was being honest, he wasn't sure he could ever step foot in his house again if it meant looking at the kitchen. He wondered if anyone had bothered cleaning up the grapes. Did they expect him to do that? His mother's stuff would be everywhere too—her purse, her clothes, her shoes—

memories of the person she had once been. What would they do with it all? Billie would just leave it because throwing it out would mean admitting she was gone. Fred, on the other hand, would want to get rid of it immediately. It was just the type of person he was. It would be how he coped. The thought made Bill sick. He ran to the bathroom and heaved up his pathetic breakfast of burnt toast into the toilet. The tears came next. He wished his mother was here to rub his back, whisper *rose petals,* and remind him that everything was okay.

When Bill returned, his brother was pacing in front of the bench.

"Billie!" Fred shouted. "They're arresting Frank. They are charging him with manslaughter." His breaths came in excited gasps.

"Manslaughter?" The word sounded too horrible to be paired with his mother.

"The jury still has to convict him. His prints were all over that knife and combined with his history of aggression… I think it's a sure thing."

A wild grin spread across Fred's face. Given the circumstances, Bill found it unnerving. For a moment, he wanted to sprint back into the bathroom and throw up a second time.

"They are going to transfer him to a facility across state. He'll stay there until the trial."

Trial. It was another word that left Bill's nerves on edge. He wasn't sure why. Of course, there would be a trial. His mother did not have the fortune of dying peacefully in her sleep, she died with a goddamn knife sticking out of her throat.

"I need to sign some paperwork. It should only take a few minutes," Fred said. "After that, we can go home."

His brother disappeared down the hall. Bill stood unmoving, trying to comprehend how this could be happening to him. How exactly he came to be standing in the middle of a police station listening to his brother talk about trials and manslaughter.

His brother seemed to think Frank being found guilty was a no brainer. Bill hoped so. His stepfather's prints on the murder weapon sure were damning enough. But then again, Bill had been there when it happened. He had watched Frank sink to his knees and caress his mother's corpse. He touched everything, including the knife, Bill was sure of it. Would the jury believe that was the only time Frank had handled the weapon that day? Could he get off? Would he plead insanity, not guilty? As his brother had said, there was also Frank's history of aggression. That alone could prove he was capable of something as horrendous and cold as murder. Bill was surprised to find a hysterical chuckle inching up his throat. History of aggression. That was a term that should only be used for stray dogs, not for a human being. Not somebody that was supposed to be a loving husband and surrogate father to two boys.

There was commotion behind him as a door swung open. Yelling and cussing bellowed down the hall. Bill recognized it as belonging to Frank. He pivoted to find his stepfather being escorted down the hall. Frank's hands were secured in cuffs, a police officer flanking him on either side. Their eyes locked.

"Billie, you little shit!" Frank screamed. "Tell them I'm innocent. Tell them I wasn't even there when you came home."

Bill said nothing. He was shocked by his stepfather's appearance. It had only been twenty-four hours, but his stepfather looked thinner. Pale. Sick. His clothes were wrinkled, his hair disheveled, his eyes rimmed a bright red. He'd been crying.

"I'm innocent!" Frank shrieked.

Bill was reminded of all the times Frank had hit his mother. "You are not innocent," Bill shouted back.

Frank glared at him. "Where is Fred? Fred will tell them. I went to get booze. I wasn't even home."

"Sir," one of the officers prompted, "if you can get yourself under control, we'll allow you to say goodbye to your son."

Frank laughed. "He is *not* my son." The officers urged Frank forward. "He's just some one-night stand's bastard. At least, Freddy's dad stuck around for a few years."

Bill wanted to tackle Frank to the ground and wrap his hands around his fat throat. But what good would that do? It would only get him locked up in a cell of his own. Wouldn't that be cute? Adjoining stepfather-son cells. Maybe they'd get the family discount at the commissary. Bill watched his stepfather continue down the hall, struggling against the guards, spitting profanities.

Fred emerged from one of the offices just as Frank rounded the corner.

"Jesus. What was all that racket?" he asked.

"Frank," Bill responded dully.

Fred shook his head in disapproval. He gave Bill a soft smile and slung an arm around his shoulders. "Come on, kid. Let's get out of here."

Bill realized then his brother was far stronger than he'd ever be. Fred coped better. He would never succumb to the temptation of blood like Bill had. Why couldn't he be more like Fred? Was it because they had different fathers? He supposed it didn't matter, Fred would always be his true brother. They had the goodness of their mother in common after all.

CHAPTER 31

Clare

My cellphone blares. My eyes pop open. I am in my room, sprawled across the comforter I hadn't bothered to turn down and crawl beneath. My old poetry books surround me like an army of enemy soldiers. A half-finished pint of tequila and the book of darkness rests next to my cheek. The word 'guilty' is printed across its exposed page. I fling the book aside and bring the phone to my ear.

"Hello?"

"Clarice? Oh, thank God."

"Erin? What's—"

"It's Mia. Somebody took Mia," she spurts through choked sobs.

I sit up. My eyes find the alarm clock on my bureau: 7:05 a.m. "What?" I ask.

"I'm such an idiot. I should have checked on her last night. If I'd check... then maybe... maybe I would have been able to stop it."

"Erin, slow down. Tell me what's going on?" I am already up. Clamping the cellphone between my ear and shoulder, I pull on pants.

"Maggie saw a man in Mia's room last night. He told her to go back to sleep. He said he needed her sister so... so...

that he could live. What does that even mean?" Erin sobs. "Maggie said he looked familiar. Do you think it could be somebody we know?"

My fingers curl around my comforter. I envision Billie on top of it as we kiss. I see him running out the door in a wild frenzy. Then I picture Frank, the things he proclaimed, the voice message my mother had left about Matt Myers—now Mia was missing. It was too coincidental. I could no longer make up any more believable excuses.

"The police say it's usually somebody we know. Oh God! Who would do this?" she asks again.

I make up these stupid rules. I don't want to hurt women or children. Wasn't that what Billie had said when he showed up at my apartment that night? I assumed he had been rambling, upset about his brother, but he had been trying to tell me he needed help, and I didn't listen. Maybe if I had, things would be different.

"Clarice?" Erin's voice shrieks on the other end.

"I'll get her back," I say before hanging up the phone.

CHAPTER 32

Billie

I have paced the wooded boundary of my parking spot nearly a hundred times. I have walked into the forest, skirted the body of a dead raccoon, and walked back out. I have splashed my face with water from the stream. Nothing helps. I cannot take it anymore. The child's cries are maddening. She had woken almost thirty minutes ago when morning light penetrated the car windows. I have tried comforting the toddler, but I don't dare take her outside for fear she will wake Gus and Darlene.

"Shush," I hush to her in the backseat. The child pauses briefly, then begins her incessant wailing once more. *What have I done?* I could bring her back. I could leave her outside a fire department. But what if they find me? All it takes is for one person to see the child in my car. Then, the police could run the plates. They'd find my brother, creating a bread crumb trail back to me.

The child lets out a shrill squeal that pierces my brain. I grab my head. I cannot think. I heave open the car door and snort a generous inhale of fresh air. I shut the door behind me and lock the child inside, making sure the windows are cracked the tiniest bit.

My stomach gurgles, and I feel the Other inching its way up to the forefront of my consciousness. Soon it will take over, and the child will not stand a chance. I cannot do this. This is *not* me.

I do not hurt children.

I do not hurt children.

I do not hurt children.

I turn and sprint into the forest.

CHAPTER 33

Twelve Years Ago

The trial had been heart-wrenching. People who had known Bill's mother took the stand. Himself. Fred. Ed from the bar. They shared tearful stories of the terrifying abuse his mother had endured. Most of their neighbors had shown up at the courthouse for support. They observed the case with growing horror, never truly aware of what went on behind closed doors. Clarice and her parents were there almost every day. Clarice seemed to watch the events unfold numb and unblinking.

When Frank took the stand and talked about his wife, he cried, his nose dripping with snot. He accused Billie of murder. When that didn't work, he tried implicating Fred. Despite his weak alibi (an old lady who checked him out at the liquor store), despite his fingerprints on the murder weapon, and despite his history of violence, his stepfather maintained his innocence.

At the end of it all, Frank was found guilty and sentenced to twelve years in Berlin Federal Correctional Institution in Berlin, New Hampshire. People applauded, lawyers shook hands, and friends doled out congratulatory hugs. Bill, however, could not smile. His stepfather's sentencing was a small win, but it would not bring his mother back and without her, he felt empty and alone.

He was not entirely alone, though. He had the Other inside him. The Other pleaded and begged to be let out. Bill had stopped eating most food because it made him sick, but the Other was always hungry. It was hungry even now as he stood in front of his house with his brother. Overwhelming dread consumed him. It was like unseen phantoms pushed on his chest with heavy hands. He did not want to step through that front door.

Bill had been staying at the apartment Fred shared with his roommate while the trial was ongoing. He liked being close to his brother even if the apartment was small and tensions were high. Now that the court had made their decision, it was expected that Billie and his brother would move on with their lives. The first step was to retrieve some of Billie's belongings from the house. They would worry about what to do with the property later.

Fred unlocked the front door and stepped inside. He did not waver, did not hesitate. It was another reminder of how brave he was. Bill wished he could be only half the man his brother was. Then again, Fred did not see what Bill had in the kitchen. Maybe if he did, he wouldn't be quite so eager to go inside.

The kitc1hen's open entryway called to Bill. It was like a bad car accident. You didn't want to see the tragedy but, at the same time, you couldn't look away. The scene had been cleaned. There were no green grapes scattered across the living room. No pool of blood on the kitchen's linoleum floor. Yet, memories of the incident remained. A fragment of yellow police tape clung to the living room baseboard. Bill imagined what it must have been like—the powder sprinkled throughout the house to test for fingerprints, the swabs and vials to collect evidence, the crew of gloved personnel walking in and out of *his* home.

Suddenly, his heart was in his throat, or was it something else? The *other* thing inside him trying to work its way out. It had grown restless and bored of his heartbreak.

"Go grab some stuff," Fred urged him.

Bill nodded and traveled down the hall almost at a sprint. He choked back hysterical sobs as he passed his mother's bedroom. *Why hadn't she listened to him? Why had she insisted on staying with Frank?*

Bill dug through his dresser drawers and shoved wrinkled clothes into his suitcase. He grabbed a couple paperbacks, a few CDs, and his deodorant from the bathroom. He paused, studying the orange pill bottles lined up in the medicine cabinet. The psychiatrists would be angry if he stopped taking his meds. Bill left them behind.

His brother was sitting on the stained sofa, flipping through an old magazine. "You ready?" he asked.

Bill nodded. His eyes bounced to the kitchen entryway then to Frank's keys on the end table. He could not be in this house. He could not be in this town. It was all too much. Now that the trial was over, what was he supposed to do? Did everyone really expect him to go back to school? Maybe take the SAT's and apply to colleges. What happens when Fred notices the neighborhood cats are disappearing? What happens when Fred catches him bent over a dead animal as his mother had?

Fred moved for the front door. "Wait," Bill blurted. "I forgot something."

His brother sighed. "Make it snappy."

Bill snatched Frank's keys off the end table. "I love you, Freddy," he said.

"What's up with you today?" Fred asked, but Bill was already at the backslider. He threw it open and ran to Frank's old Toyota in the driveway. He tossed his suitcase on the passenger seat and started the car with trembling hands. *It's better like this*, he reminded himself. *Fred will be safer.*

He did not look back, even as Fred ran out on the front steps screaming for him to stop.

. . .

Billie was in some unknown town more than two hours from Wolfeboro. He had been idling in the Toyota for over three hours in a state park bordering a thick forest. He watched the sky transform from an orange glow to an inky purple. All the while, his stomach growled.

A man pulled in next to him. He exited his truck wearing a thin sweatshirt and athletic shorts. A jogger, Bill presumed. There were lots of them here. They ran the wooded trails alone, sometimes with their dogs. Most of them had left an hour ago when twilight descended.

The new jogger strapped a headlamp to his forehead and took off down one of the trails. The Other awakened, coiling in the back of Bill's throat. Seconds turned into minutes, and twilight succumbed to full darkness. Only the jogger's truck remained in the parking lot. Everyone else had vacated the park, returning to their families. If only Bill had a family to go back to. He pushed images of his brother from his mind. Fred was strong. He would be fine without him, happier even.

Bill caught sight of the jogger's headlamp bouncing in the darkness as he navigated the trail back towards his truck. Bill's breath caught in his throat. The Other fidgeted. Killing cats was one thing but killing a man was another. He swallowed hard. *Was that what he was doing here? Killing a man? Just a brief pit-stop on his road trip, kind of like stopping at a roadside McDonald's when you're hungry.* Bill longed to start the Toyota and speed away, but the Other was too strong, too present. Bill's jaw clicked. His stomach ached with hunger. As the jogger inched closer, his heart accelerated to a heart attack rhythm. He reached for the door handle.

What was he doing? What was he doing? What in the hell was he doing?

Bill's feet hit the grass and advanced towards the innocent man.

Stop. Stop. Stop.

The jogger's back was to Billie, his keys in one hand, ready to call it a night after a long day at work. Bill reached out, grabbing him by the shoulder.

No. No. No.

But it was too late. All Billie saw was swirling black. He didn't even hear the man cry out. He only felt the rush of hot blood as it splashed onto his face.

The Other drank.

CHAPTER 34

Clare

The car lurches to a stop in front of the white farmhouse. An uprising of dirt rises around it. Gus and Darlene are on the porch in their adjacent rocking chairs. Darlene stands as I open the car door.

"Oh, it's Clare," she says to Gus.

"Is Billie here?" I ask.

"I'm not sure. It's his day off." Gus replies.

"He hasn't been up to the house yet," Darlene interjects.

"If he is here," Gus says, "he'll be down at the store in his room. I'll walk you there. Store's locked up, don't open for another half hour."

Gus rises and hobbles down the porch steps. We descend the hill at a much slower pace than I like. Gus unlocks the front door, and we step inside.

"His room's just back there," Gus says, motioning towards the far end of the little store.

I follow his direction and head for the hallway between the freezers. The door to Billie's room is shut. I pound on it. "Billie! Open up!"

I pause, listening for the shuffling of feet on the other side. I pray he will answer the door and tell me this has all been some big misunderstanding. He doesn't kill people. He doesn't steal children.

"Open up!" I shout again.

After no response, I try the handle. It's unlocked. The door opens to reveal the smallest room I have ever seen. It is empty. The cot made up. Clothes put away in the small bureau. There is no sign suggesting Billie spent the night.

"He's not here," I shout to Gus. "Fuck, he's not here," I mutter to myself. I push past the old man and race up the hill. Darlene drops her crochet and jumps to her feet when she spots me.

"Is everything okay?"

"Billie's gone," I huff between gulps of air. "I think… I think he's done something horrible."

Darlene's hand flutters to her face, covering her open mouth. "What do you mean?" she asks, but I am already sprinting down the long driveway to the spot Billie parks his car.

I enter the tree line slowly. I do not want to spook him. Avoiding the crunch of leaves and twigs, I creep forward. The Toyota is just ahead. The sunlight bounces off one of the windows reflecting into the trees. I hold my breath, listening. Muffled crying comes from the direction of the car.

Mia.

I dash forward, pausing briefly to scan for Billie.

Nothing.

I approach the Toyota preparing myself for what I might see. Mia's throat cut. The car seat stained with bright red blood. Or maybe Billie's head blown off, a handgun resting in one hand.

I peer through the back window. The toddler is standing on the back seat, supporting herself with the headrest. She faces the rear windshield, tears streaming down her rosy cheeks. I breathe out a sigh of relief. She is okay.

"Hey, little girl," I coo.

Mia's head tilts towards me, and she curls her fingers into a little wave.

The windows are cracked just enough to let in some air. Billie wouldn't leave her in the car for long. "I'm going to get you out of there," I promise.

CHAPTER 35

Billie

I want to run until I'll never be found again, but I am too weak. Needing some sort of nourishment, my legs propel me to the dead raccoon I spotted earlier. Its carcass is relatively fresh. The signs of decay are minimum. It appears no other animals have feasted on the creature. You would think that'd be a good sign, but it could also mean the coon is infected with rabies. Animals have the innate ability to sense those kinds of things. Lacking even the sense of an animal, the Other does not care.

I fall to my knees before the carcass and feed. The clotted liquid is hot from the sun. The dark red, almost black blood lacks vitality. It tastes stale. I chuckle, feeling the last of my sanity slip away. Stale is a word used to describe long-forgotten Wonder Bread not the insides of a dead raccoon.

The Other has its fill. My stomach is plump with the heavy liquid. I toss the carcass aside, halfheartedly wipe the blood from my mouth, and stand. My head spins and spots flash before my eyes. I trudge back towards the car, the carpet of dead leaves crunching with each step. I feel no relief from the feed. In fact, I feel worse. My heartbeat thumps in my ears. My forehead is cold and slick with sweat. A sickening gurgle thunders from my gut as stomach acid pools in the back of my throat.

Vile.

The blood did not just taste stale, it tasted absolutely vile. My stomach lurches, and I vomit. The blood I just consumed reappears in a sickening red splatter across the forest floor. I go to stand, pause, then throw up again. More rejected blood materializes, more energy wasted. It is on my third heave I realize this didn't work. My last attempt to satisfy the Other has failed.

My eyes feel sunken in a skull that seems too large for my slender body. A body that, at this point, is not much more than skin draped across bones. I am starving to death. I need to eat something, and it is waiting for me back at the car.

Through the trees, I spot someone idling by the Toyota. My heart accelerates from a slow trot to a full gallop. Crouching, I push forward and inch myself closer. It's Clarice. She has her hands cupped around the rear window.

Damnit.

She must have figured out my secret and, if she hasn't, the sight of her crying cousin locked in my back seat will surely confirm her worst fears. The police could be here any second to haul me away. I will die in prison. I will never be able to sustain my life source without blood. No one will understand.

Clare's hand is on the door handle now, yanking it with full force. The toddler is crying. I curse under my breath. Why Clarice? Why did you have to show up now? I wish you could have just left it alone.

CHAPTER 36

Clare

Tugging on the door handle is useless. My eyes scan the forest floor and land on a decent-sized rock. It will have to do. I slam it against the Toyota's passenger side window as hard as I can. The force sends vibrations up my forearm. My efforts yield only a thin crack unlike the explosion of glass I had hoped for.

"Mom-me," the toddler says and lets out a horrible, heart-wrenching screech.

I secure my grip around the stone and go at it again, striking the glass over and over. The small line crackles and expands outwards into thin branches. One more hit should…

"I'm sorry," I hear from behind me, then I am falling forward. A loud bang is followed by a blinding pain in my forehead. Glittering spots consume my vision, the edges darkening. I feel dirt and grass beneath me. I am on the ground.

"Fuck," I say. I sit up and rub my head. My palm comes away clean. Footsteps pad around the car, followed by the release of the mechanical door locks. Mia is still screeching.

"Wait, Billie," I try to mutter, but the pounding in my head makes me wonder if I even said the words out loud. I take a deep breath. The spots and darkness lessen.

"Please, don't follow me," he says. "Just leave this alone."

I look up in time to see Billie whirl around and take off towards the tree line, Mia snug in his arms. I maneuver onto my hands and knees.

Someone else steps in front of me, blocking my line of sight.

"Clare?"

Gus's wrinkled face peers down at me. "I saw him hit you. What's happening? What's going on?" His voice rises in decibels and urgency.

"He will kill her," I say.

With that, Gus wheels around. I realize then he is holding a pistol. He raises it to the sky and fires. The shot echoes through the forest. Nearby birds squawk and flutter into the sky. Mia lets out a shrill scream of terror. Billie freezes.

"Drop the girl, Billie," Gus commands.

Billie sets Mia on the ground. Gus rushes forward and tackles Billie to the forest floor. The two bodies partake in a struggle. Mia crawls from them, releasing another scream. Gus manages to punch Billie square in the face, and he lays still. Billie is weak, nothing more than a skeleton, it didn't take much.

I attempt to rise. Stars swarm my vision and send me right back to my knees.

"Are you okay?" Gus asks, hobbling towards me.

"I nod. "Where's Mia?"

"She's fine. She's by the car."

"Bring her back to—"

Billie is up, running unsteadily towards Mia.

"Gus!" I cry.

He spins around, fumbling for the pistol. He raises it to the air again and shoots. The sound of the blast reverberates into my brain, causing my ears to ring. Mia screams. This time, Billie doesn't stop, perhaps calling Gus's bluff. He sprints into the woods. I'll lose them forever if I don't move *now*.

"Run. Go get help," I spit at Gus. He obeys, retreating towards his house.

Using the car door handle, I hoist myself to my feet. A jab of pain nearly brings me to my knees again. Another deep breath and I am walking. I focus on putting one foot in front of the other until I manage a slow jog. I follow Billie into the woods.

Mia's cries carry through the quiet forest. I pick up the pace following the sound like a dog trailing a scent. The dots before my eyes subside. Only a dull ache remains where my head must have struck the side of the car. I push my legs harder despite my screaming lungs and protesting body.

"Billie!" I shout, my voice cracking.

He does not respond, but Mia does by releasing another high-pitched wail.

"Quiet, dammit." Billie's reprimand echoes off the trees.

I pause. They are close. I follow Billie's hurried footsteps. Pumping my arms and legs harder, I weave through the tangles of saplings and briars. A branch snags my hair shooting fresh pain to my injured skull. Light filters through the canopy. The trees are thinning. I struggle to maintain my balance as I navigate large rocks and fallen pines. Then, a new sound presents among the child's howls and the rustle of leaves. A powerful sound. The rush of water.

I summon my last bit of strength and burst through the foliage into a clearing. The scene I discover is one I could not have prepared for. Billie is standing maybe ten feet away with Mia clutched to his chest like a madman, a box cutter in one hand. A waterfall cascades from a tall cliff behind them into an unseen valley below.

"Stop running," I heave between gulps of air even though I know the words are pointless as soon as they leave my mouth. My eyes dart to the treetops behind Billie. Judging by their height, only a few inches are separating him from a fatal drop. Running would be pointless. Impossible.

I give Billie a quick once over. He looks worse than the last time I saw him. His skin is a sickly pale exacerbating the black circles beneath his eyes. The same eyes, that only a few days ago, I had gazed into before kissing are now wild and crazed. He resembles more of a frightened animal than human. More monster, than friend. He is almost unrecognizable. His lips are tainted by a reddish-black smear.

Mia seems unharmed. She smiles at the sight of me. The only evidence she's been crying are the two rivers of tear stains that mark her flushed cheeks.

"You can end this right now, Billie. Just bring me Mia, and we can get out of here," I say while trying to steady my voice.

"It doesn't work like that, Clarice. I can't *just* end this," Billie responds. "I need to do this. I need to if I am going to live. If it's not Mia, it will just be some other child."

"I know you, Billie. This isn't you. You don't hurt children. This—"

"I'm a monster!" he screams.

"No, you're not." Although the statement sounds unconvincing even to my own ears. "You are just confused. We can get you help."

He shakes his head. "I killed my own mother, Clarice. I fucking killed her. Who does that?" Tears stream down his face. "It doesn't matter what I do now. I have no morals. No rules. It's all bullshit."

"No," I said. "You did not kill your mother."

"You don't know that."

"Your fingerprints weren't on the knife."

"That means nothing."

"She'd been dead for over an hour when you found her."

"Maybe I blacked out."

"No. The timeline's wrong."

Say it then. Say it, Clarice. Tell the fucking truth for once in your life.

"I found her first," Billie says. "I was the only one home—"

"I did," I blurt. "I killed her." I feel my face redden as the blood rushes from my racing heart to my head.

He snorts a laugh. "No. No. No. Don't say that. Don't try to make me feel better."

"I killed her," I repeat.

"Why are you saying that?" he roars. His voice bounces off the rocks and seems to shake the woods around us.

I take a deep breath. "When I was fourteen, Frank raped me. I hated him, and I swore I'd never let it happen again." Now, hot tears well in my eyes. "That day, I got locked out of my house, so I went to your place. Frank's car wasn't in the driveway, and I didn't know where else to go. I was desperate. You weren't home from school yet. Fred let me in. He had to go to work and told me I could stay as long as I needed. My dad was going to be home in ten minutes. A few minutes later, I heard keys in the front door. I thought it was Frank, and I panicked."

Billie stares back at me with such intensity it makes me want to look away. I hold his gaze.

"I ran into the kitchen, grabbed a knife, and pressed my back against the wall nearest the door. I pictured him touching me again. I remembered the feeling of his hands on me and not being strong enough to do anything about it. I couldn't let that happen again. Do you understand that?"

Billie is silent.

"When I heard footsteps enter the kitchen, I just swung. I didn't know… I didn't expect it to be your mom."

The tears explode down my face now. I bring my hands to my mouth fearing I might throw up. I see *her* expression then, her eyes wide as her trembling fingers find the handle of the knife submerged in her neck. "I couldn't move. I couldn't think. Calling for help never even crossed my mind. Instead, I sunk into the corner and watched her die," I croak through sobs.

Billie shakes his head.

"The next thing I know, I hear someone in the living room. The thought of Frank got me up, and I ran to the far end of the kitchen and hid behind the basement door. But it was you, Billie. I heard you scream. I heard you cry, and still, I did nothing. I escaped through one of the basement windows after Frank arrived. I heard the sirens as I rounded the corner to my house." I pause to take a deep breath. "I'm sorry, Billie. I have lived with this secret every day. Every time I find happiness, I push it away. I don't deserve it. Not after what I did. That's why I got this tattoo." I push back my sleeve, revealing *never forget who you really are* printed in black ink. "Every single time I look at this, I remember what I did. What I am. That's why I want you to stop. You are better than this. You did not hurt your mom. Let your conscious at least be free of that."

"No. You're lying," he says.

"I am not lying. Why would I—"

"Because you want me to feel better. Because you want to protect me for some reason that I cannot even begin to understand. Your lies don't change things." He raises the box cutter to the child's throat.

"Rose petals!" I scream.

"Wha—what did you say?"

"Rose petals."

"How—"

"It's what you said to your mother when you found her in the kitchen."

Billie is silent. His face somehow turns paler than it already is.

"I told you it was me," I say. "I'm a monster too."

CHAPTER 37

Billie

Rose petals. The word vibrates through my skull, nearly causing me to stumble back and drop the child. The box cutter slips from my hand, clattering to the ground. It is impossible. How could Clare know those words? How could she know the secret shared only between me and my mother? Is she telling the truth? Had Clarice really killed her?

This time my knees do buckle. I take a step back, and my foot flirts with the edge of the cliff. I steady myself and secure my hold on the child. I feel like bursting into tears and screaming at the top of my lungs. For a moment, I think I might, if only to relieve the heaviness in my chest.

"You killed my mother," I say more to hear it aloud than to Clarice.

She nods, more tears spew down her face. "I'm sorry," she whispers through sobs. "I am so sorry, Billie."

"Frank is innocent," I say.

"He is far from innocent," she responds firmly.

For eleven years, the police and the people of Wolfeboro have been deceived. Frank is not a murderer. All those times he had proclaimed his innocence, he had been telling the truth. But Frank had been wrong about that day too. I did not kill my mother—Clarice did. My neighbor. My best friend. The woman I love.

"You… you… should have called for help. Maybe you could have saved her," I choke out between sobs.

"I know," she cries.

The brief moment of relief I felt for not being responsible for my mother's murder is soon overcome by horrible anger and a desperate hunger. The Other has woken. It craves my rage and sadness.

It creeps from my stomach, up my esophagus, and to the back of my throat. I want to choke it down. I want to rip it out, slam it to the ground, and set it on fire. But, sadly, it is a part of me. A part that cannot be severed. My mother always said that I was special, maybe this is what she meant. I picture her now. What she would say if she was here. I know she would not want me to hurt this child. She had raised two herself with the help of no husband. I set Mia down and give her a nudge towards Clarice, desiring to be the man my mother wanted me to be.

"Thank you, Billie," Clarice says with a soft smile, her blue eyes glistening.

The Other does not like that I sent the child away. It was hoping for an easy meal. A meal that would heal us. I grab my neck, attempting to hold it in.

"Billie?" Clarice whelps, shielding the toddler behind her legs.

The Other slithers to the front of my mouth. My neck and shoulders crunch and crack as it possesses me. My head jerks back at a painful angle. My jawbone widens and extends. Dozens of long, black fangs shoot painfully through my gums, crowding between my teeth. My head snaps forward. My eyes lock onto Clarice, the woman I somehow continue to love despite everything she has done to me.

"Billie?" she screams, her voice strangled with terror, her eyes wide with horror.

I want to run to her and hold her tight, but the monster wants me to tear her throat out and drink her blood. The Other desires to rip each of her pretty limbs from their sockets and chew on her milk-white bones.

"Run," I command.

She shakes her head.

"Run!" I scream.

"No. This isn't you, Billie."

The statement stuns me. I envision my brother punching me and smiling from across the table. My mother coming home late from the bar and tucking me into bed. I remember climbing the oak tree with Clarice. I feel my hands on her body as we kiss in her dark room. I shake my head. She is right. This isn't me. I can be better than this.

"Rose petals," I say to myself. Then, I turn and jump.

CHAPTER 38

Clare

One second Billie is standing in front of me with his mouth wide and filled with black needle fangs—the next he is gone. I scream and rush forward even though I know it's too late. There is nothing I can do. I peer over the cliff anyway, hoping he will be there clinging to a loose root or branch. Instead, I see the outline of his motionless form sixty feet below. His limbs are sprawled at unnatural angles, his head surrounded by sharp, jagged rocks.

I stumble back from the edge. An animalistic cry escapes me. I bury my head into my hands. I thought after confessing to Billie that all the tears in my body had dried up. I was wrong. They spew forth in such a frightening intensity, it is difficult to catch my breath between sobs.

Mia lets out a concerned coo behind me. I return to the toddler, scoop her up, and hold her close. The wind carries the approaching sound of sirens. I collapse to my knees, Mia still cradled in my arms, and succumb to more tears.

I listen to the commotion in the woods behind me. There is yelling, hurried footsteps pushing through the foliage, and the concerned barking of dogs. Darlene and Gus spot me in the clearing a few moments later. "She's over here! Over here!" Gus yells.

Soon there is a crowd of emergency response personnel around me. Darlene rushes to my side. She caresses my head and wiggles Mia from my lifeless arms. I remain slouched on the ground until two paramedics hoist me to my feet. They seat me on a log, wrap a blanket around my shoulders, and tend to my head injury while offering me water and kind words. I decline both, preferring to sit in silence and stare into the distance as they do a quick examination.

The police come next. They divide into smaller teams. One group, with two German Shepherds, descend the cliff as the other surveys the top. They examine the ground where Billie and I had been standing, probably looking for clues. Maybe signs of a struggle. Two suits, one male, the other female, appear in front of me.

"Clarice," the female officer says. Her voice is soft and gentle. She must be a mother. "My name is Agent Bates. This is Agent Grady," she says, gesturing to the short, stocky man beside her. "We are with the FBI." She flashes her badge. "We need to ask you a few questions. Is that okay?"

I nod. My throat goes cotton dry, and I wish I had accepted the water the paramedics had offered.

The male agent says, "We are told your friend kidnapped a toddler—"

"My cousin."

"Yes, your cousin, Mia," the female agent says. "Then there was a struggle, and you ran after him?"

I nod again.

"Based on the 911 call and what your friends have told us." He hooks a thumb back at Gus and Darleen. "We have an inkling of who your friend might be," the male agent says.

Say it then, I want to scream. *Say that he is The New Hampshire Vampire.*

"We discovered a suit coat buried a couple of miles from a crime scene behind The Woodline Pub," he continues. "Witnesses claim Billie was wearing it the night Matt Myers was murdered. They also said there was an altercation between Matt and Billie, and that you were with him that night at The Woodline Pub. It's only a matter of time until the lab finds something on the jacket. That being said, we are not accusing you of anything. We just want to know what happened after you followed Billie here."

"He just jumped," I say.

"Was there a physical altercation?"

"No."

"How did you get that?" The female agent asks, gesturing to the gash across my forehead.

I shrug. "Must have got it running through the woods."

"Excuse me, Grady, Bates. Can I have a quick word?" a cop asks. He motions the officers away from me, and they discuss something in a hushed huddle. Grady and Bates nod their heads in unison and return to where I am seated.

"We just want to clarify your statement one more time, Clarice," the female agent says. "Are you sure that's what happened? That he jumped?"

I nod and cradle my head in my hands as I recall Billie leaping from the cliff. It was nothing like cartoons depict. He didn't walk a few paces, look down, make a funny face, and fall with the sound of a missile trailing behind him. No, there were no Bugs Bunny antics, just a sudden, life-ending drop.

The male agent coughs uncomfortably like he is trying to elicit attention to make a toast. "We just received word from our people on the ground," he begins. "They're reporting there is no sign of a body."

I snap my head up. "What?"

"If your friend jumped from that height, he would be…" he trails off.

I finish his sentence in my head. If my friend jumped from that height, he would be dead. Caput. Splat.

The female agent places a hand on my shoulder. "Sometimes, during stressful situations, things can become kind of fuzzy. We might think we saw something when we didn't."

Vampires aren't just scary stories. They can be real, Frank whispers in my head. I relive the image I will never be able to forget. Billie's head cranked back at an impossible angle. The monstrous growls he'd made as those black, rotting fangs appeared in his mouth. His eyes had transformed into an inky black as his pupils expanded. But the worst of it had been the muted glow shining from the back of his throat, almost as if something else was inside him trying to get out.

Frank and Eve had been wrong. Billie was never sick. He didn't have Renfield Syndrome or Clinical Vampirism or any other disorder. It all makes perfect sense now. "I guess there wouldn't be a body," I say.

The FBI agents lean forward.

I study the outline of my tattoo. "Not if he's a monster."

The agents stare at me with expressions of disbelief and annoyance. I don't expect anything different. They did not see what I had. They couldn't even imagine it in their wildest fantasies.

"There is something I need to confess," I begin. "Eleven years ago, I did something horrible."

A NOTE FROM THE AUTHOR

Renfield Syndrome, aka Clinical Vampirism, is a disorder not accepted (yet) by the Diagnostic and Statistical Manual of Mental Disorders, 5th Edition (DSM-5) despite reports dating back to the late 1800s. Therefore, no person can officially be diagnosed with Renfield Syndrome.

I came across Renfield Syndrome while completing my psychology degree. The little talked about disorder always fascinated me. Although much of the ideology mentioned in this story is based on various research I've read throughout the years, this is a fictional story which by no means is an accurate portrayal of this disorder. Furthermore, the violence in this book is exaggerated and not something that is typically seen in individuals suspected of having Renfield Syndrome. The fact is, this disorder is rare and will need to be studied further if it is ever to appear in the DSM.

While researching this book, it was also inevitable that I came across people that engage in the "vampire lifestyle". From what I've learned there can be many types of "vampires" including those who feed off energy. Those who engage in modern vampirism are not synonymous with having Renfield Syndrome. There is an ample amount of resources on the great worldwide web for those of you who are interested in learning more. I want to make it clear that the intentions behind my story are pure, and I do not wish to offend anyone of the vampire community.

Thanks for reading.
This book is vampire friendly.

J.M. White

Word-of-mouth is crucial for any author to succeed. If you
enjoyed the book, please leave a review online—
anywhere you are able. Even if it's just a sentence or two.
It would make all the difference and would be very much
appreciated.

Thanks!
J.M.

ABOUT THE AUTHOR

J.M. White attended the University of Massachusetts Boston where she received a degree in psychology but spent most of her time reading fiction. Her first book, *Shattered,* is a paranormal domestic thriller. J.M. is also the creator of *Thirst for Thrillers,* a blog pairing books and cocktails, a concept aimed at encouraging more people to read good books in a genre she loves.

She currently lives in the greater Boston area.

Visit jmwhitefiction.com for more.